High Tide

Where life is a game, meant to be watched and everyone is a part of it.

SANYA PIRANI

PUBLISHED BY

SIGMA'S BOOKSHELF

MINNETONKA, MN 55305
WWW.SIGMASBOOKSHELF.COM

High Tide

Printed in the United States of America

First Printing 2023

ISBN 978-1-959538-01-1

Chapter One

Dearest Mia

April

Mia is my name. A simple, common name suited for a simple, common person, who is not good enough to be part of this family. My foster mom is a straitlaced woman and is the exact opposite of me. In her mind, everything has to be perfect. I rolled my eyes at the thought of my foster mom as I entered the house and locked the white door, then ran up to my room.

When I got there, I plopped down on the bed and smiled. Not because I was happy or anything, but because I had a roof over my head. My room is pretty small, but big enough I guess. I have a small cherry colored desk that looks more like a table, the chair I was sitting in, a silver laptop with a yellow, fabric case, and my unmade bed.

I looked out the window just as Spencer reached my foster mom's house, and smiled. Spencer has been my best friend pretty much since I ended up here. He's like an older, protective brother to me. He always makes sure that I'm safe, and checks up on me every so often to make sure I didn't fall into a black hole or something.

I sprang off the bed and ran downstairs, just as Spencer was knocking at the door.

"Hi Spence. Come on in," I said, holding the door open

for him. He came in, dropped his backpack by the door, then sat down. I watched him as he pulled apart the white laces on his Air Force Ones.

"You don't have to do that," I said. "My foster mother isn't here."

"Yes I do," said Spencer, who always was a rule follower, so I let it go. Once he had his shoes off and placed his shoes by the door, I started making my way into the living room and into my room, expecting him to follow me. "What are you doing? Thinking again?" he asked.

"I'm always thinking," I sighed, not bothering to turn around. "What do you think I am? A rock?"

Spencer laughed, but then his voice turned serious, "I didn't mean it like that." Spencer has been my so-called best friend since second grade and his family has been like a second family to me. While most of the kids at school tend to ignore him because they think he's a nerd, I really appreciate his intellect. He's a natural genius who I am pretty sure gets his smarts from his mom; and his good looks definitely come from his dad. Like his dad, Spencer has dark, almost black hair with a tint of auburn. That's not all that makes him stand out. His eyes flare pure green, unlike any eye color I've seen before. Today, he was wearing fashionable, black denim with a white shirt and kept perfect posture.

"What are you doing here anyway?" I asked as I turned myself, not the four-wheeled chair I was sitting in.

Unamused, Spencer responded, "Are we playing twenty questions or something?"

I give a half smile, but no response came out of my partially open mouth.

"What are *you* doing anyway?" Spencer wondered out loud, looking around at my messy room. There was dirty laundry on the floor at the foot of my bed, and the yellow and orange quilted bedspread hung off the side, practically on the floor too. Like most days, I hadn't bothered to make my bed.

It took me a couple seconds to answer his question. "Thinking. Just thinking."

"Well, then I'll be going. I was just checking to make sure you were okay. I was passing by anyway," Spencer said.

"You always pass by. You're my neighbor," I reminded as he left my room.

Once I heard footsteps creaking down the stairs, I got up, walked to the doorway, and watched Spencer make his way down the stairs, then open the front door and leave. *Okay, now what?* I thought. *Elaine's not even home, or is she?*

I decided to check each room for my foster mom. I felt my stomach groan out of hunger. *Where could she be?* Just when I was about to head downstairs and look there, I heard a loud crash, then a boom. I froze in place out of fear. *Be brave, Mia.* I squatted down to grab a textbook from my unusually large backpack, then while trying to stand back up tripped and fell on the carpet. I winced. Now whoever entered this house probably ran away or knew where I was.

I ignored the pain in my ankle and made my way towards the rail overlooking the living room below. I looked down and didn't see any motion in the room below, so I made my way slowly downstairs with the big book in hand. When I reached the bottom I called out, "Who's there?"

No response. I made my way over to the clear glass case where my foster mother stores the china. On the bottom of the plate closet was a broken piece of floral dinnerware. I sighed and grabbed a broom. I then swept up the mess. As I was sweeping, a piece of paper blew away from the mess. It had a coffee stain on it. I picked it up. It still smelled like old, dried up tears. I cringed at the salty smell. It was a folded piece of paper. I unfolded it and another note fell out. I caught it, letting my fingers crumple the paper. I placed the notes on the wooden table to my right. I quickly cleaned up the shattered plate and took the garbage out to the garage so that Elaine wouldn't see the china plate in the trash can.

Once the mess was cleaned up and I had put the broom back in the closet, I grabbed the notes off the table and made my way back upstairs to my room to read them.

Dear whoever finds this letter,

I'm afraid I was a part of that horrible event and it's not something I like sharing. Here goes nothing. There were two friends named Marissa and Maybelle. Marissa is known for her half bald, bright blue and green hair, while Maybelle is known for her temper. Marissa's sisters, Addy and Adaline, full of jealousy and rage, left Marissa in the cold, dark sea. They also lit Maybelle's house on fire, causing her mother to die.

Fifty years later I found a half dead girl named—as you can guess—Marissa. I let her fall into Maybelle's wrath and a long story shortened, now she is stuck up in the air for the rest of her life.

This all took place in a world called High Tide. A place you will be visiting soon for a day, if you have read this letter. In High Tide you achieve small powers that won't work once you get back on Earth, so use them carefully. Don't you fear though. Your death is your choice. Work hard to get what you want. The game is in your hands. Keep track of time. You have one day and one night to escape.

You are probably glad you had nothing to do with that now. We made terrible decisions. We

*should have known better. No, you should know
better. The things we plan don't always go as
they are supposed to. We all should know better.
Now, my advice is to take this story I have told
and make your own decisions. Maybe one day
you will help change our mistakes for the better
because we tell you history so it doesn't happen
again. We live on Earth to realize what we did
wrong. We live in High Tide to fix our mistakes.
Think smart, but don't take it too seriously. Your
thoughts can also hurt you. Don't let the challenge
get to you and remember that life is game meant
to be watched, and everyone is part of it. So play
it, don't waste it.*

Yours truly,
Nerissa

I folded up the letter and unfolded the other one. Then
I started reading.

February 2, 2013

Dearest Mia,

*I'm so very sorry. I understand that you're a
little too young to fully understand this letter, but
your grandmother is very sick. I've packed up and
will be leaving for Madison, Wisconsin tomorrow.
This is probably a very bad time to leave, noting
how old you are and how close you are to your
day at High Tide. So, I have a lot of explaining
to you before you turn twelve.*
The first thing you should know is that your

grandfather's brother, my uncle Elliot Lopez, competed in this game called the High Tide Challenge. Descendants of those who became Queens or Kings in High Tide compete in the challenge every May. It's a challenge to see if you are as brave as your ancestors.

Every year a new Queen comes to High Tide. But for fifty years the same Queens have been ruling. Elliot never finished the High Tide Challenge—like everyone else who competed— nor became a King. Elliot had a journal he wrote in during the challenge. It was found near a High Tide Exit called the Trap. Although his journal was found, no one knows where he went. He disappeared, just like everyone who enters High Tide, except, for the Queens.

I didn't give you the journal because of how much it's worth. I couldn't put you at risk of people going after you to steal Elliot's writing. Elliot was extremely close to solving the challenge, so this information could be used to your advantage when you compete in the challenge. The challenge generates obstacles to stop you from escaping. Escaping is the easiest part. Each year High Tide creates a prophecy to give you hints to escape. The Trap is the place your grandfather almost escaped from and finding your way there is the easiest way to escape.

The second thing is that there are five Queens living in High Tide. Their names are Allison, Marissa, Nerissa, Lauren, and Maybelle. Also, living in High Tide are Techs who spend their lives coding to create the obstacles in High Tide.

Third, on the back of Elliot's journal were the

*words, "Life is a game meant to be watched, and
everyone is a part of it."*

*I don't have much time 'till I have to leave,
so I'll spend some of the last words of this letter
saying that I'll miss you. I promise to visit as often
as I can and I wish you the best of luck. Good
luck, Mia.*

*Love,
Mom*

I re-read my mom's letter. I could feel salty water burn my eyes, threatening to let tears fall down. I swiftly dabbed at my glassy eyes. *Don't let anyone see you cry.* She, my mom, was planning to leave the next day anyway when she died. *Was my grandmother still sick? Why had Elaine kept this from me? Did Elliot die or just magically disappear?* I gently put the letters in my backpack.

CREAK

I heard the door to Elaine's house open.

"Sorry I am late. I got stuck in traffic. Where are you, Mia?" she called out in her monotone voice as she made her way into the house.

"I'm upstairs," I answered. "Be right down."

When I got downstairs, Elaine was sitting at the table in the living room looking at the day's mail. She straightened her black skirt and fixed her white, button-up blouse when she saw me.

"You must be hungry. I'll get you something to eat," she said, then put down the letters, got back up, and headed towards the kitchen.

I shrugged my shoulders as she straightened her skirt again and left the room. A few minutes later, she came back with a heated, microwavable dinner and a silver fork.

I peeled off the clear plastic and then took the fork and picked at the warm dinner in a plastic tray. I was hungry, but very distracted, so I put the fork down and reached for my backpack. I took out the letters. *I'm insane, I'm about to show Elaine the letters.*

"What are these? And how did you get them?" I asked.

Elaine looked up and when she realized what I was holding, frowned and said sternly, "Where did you find those?"

I shrugged and Elaine spoke again. "I asked where you found those."

I contemplated telling her the truth, but knew I'd get blamed for breaking the dish if I did, so I decided against it and instead shrugged my shoulders and said, "I'm going to bed."

"But, you didn't finish your dinner. Oh well, good night, Maya." Elaine stood up to gather the plastic dish, pushing the chair behind her against the wall.

"I didn't change my name to Maya. It's still Mia."

Elaine looked up at me and I could see she was on the verge of snapping at me. "I know. I just thought that people would be more likely to adopt you if your name didn't mean 'bitter.'"

"I haven't been adopted yet and I've been here for five years." I gave her a look, then stood up and made my way back upstairs.

Chapter Two

Stay Alive and Escape

Fast forward a day…

I groaned and glared at the book that sat on the wooden desk. The English room smelled of wood and the pages of new books. I was the last person in the stuffy, small room, but I didn't care. I just kept glowering at the old, used pages as if that was all it took to make the boring book disappear. I picked the book up and shoved it in my heavy backpack with the green and yellow swirls.

When I got to class, my teacher looked at me concerned and questioned, "Are you okay, Mia?" She wore a green, cold shoulder blouse and black pants. She wore her black hair with red highlights in a bob. Her face was covered with a lame attempt at makeup. Her eyeliner was made up of squiggly lines and her mascara leaked to her eyelids. The teacher seemed young, as if she was in her twenties or so.

"Yeah, I'm fine, Mrs. Young," I responded.

"Nerissa," she corrected.

The letter saying I would participate in High Tide was signed by a person named Nerissa. I almost dropped my textbooks after hearing her name. Nerissa was quick. From behind the desk where she was sitting, she put her hand to the side of my textbooks and stopped them from falling. I noticed her matte painted nails. They were long and were painted an ocean blue. All except for her ring finger that is. The nail at the end of it was painted sea green.

"I-I-I'm fine," I stuttered, walking towards the walnut wood doorway.

"Be careful, Mia." Nerissa looked at me awkwardly. Part of me hoped she was talking about dropping my books and not the High Tide Challenge. I hoped the letter was actually a prank. That my mom wasn't actually thinking about leaving before she died. A little part of me believed the letters I found were true.

How many Nerissa's are there in the world? Could she be the person who wrote that letter? I left and shut the brown, wooden door behind me.

I was fidgeting in my wheeled, cherry colored seat, twirling a yellow pencil in my hand. My fingers always had a need to move when I was thinking. Teachers always get on my nerves when they see me fidgeting and they call me out for "not paying attention." Like I would be paying attention if you didn't tell me to stop moving. Anyway, back to what I was thinking.

I don't know what made me think of the letter I'd found just yesterday. The one telling me in gold lettering that I would be participating in the High Tide Challenge—the one my mom left for me before she died. The one my foster mom kept hidden from me. Could it be true? I've heard stories about people who have never returned. I flicked the mechanical pencil to the wall. The High Tide Challenge was apparently a yearly event that allows people in different states and provinces to compete. Each year two of the people who have gotten a letter from each state or province can compete against the other teams. No one has ever won. It's impossible to escape.

***

I started playing with the yellow, mechanical pencil again. *Think smart, but don't take it too seriously. Your thoughts can also hurt you.* What does that even *mean?*

I have looked up High Tide. I have gleaned information. I have thought things through. They say the day you compete will be May first, and that nobody can foretell or predict when their turn will come. Even though this day would still be a mystery, everybody knew that this day could help you face your fears, and heal you. The only thing you have to do is to stay alive on that very day and escape. They say you are lucky if you get to participate in this day of courage.

As I was tapping my fingers on the desk, a curl of hair flew to my face. As I tied up my dark hair, I felt my eyelids getting heavy. I gave in and put my head down, slowly drifting into a dream. A dream about disasters, reckless happenings, and so much worse. Little did I know.

Chapter Three

Lightning

May 1st...

You wouldn't expect anything to happen at three a.m., but here I was still sitting in my seat in my room. I had been in this very spot for hours, lost in thought. I was one of those people who seem like they're staring at nothing as they lose track of their surroundings while they think.

When I finally snapped out of it, I felt my feet touch the fluffy, tan carpet and knew what I had to do. I got up, ran down the wooden stairs, quickly grabbed the strap of my backpack, then ran back to my room. I fell to the floor and started pulling things out of my backpack until I found the letters, then I went back to my desk, sat down, and reread them. My mom's letter said the High Tide Challenge was in May. Today was May first. Is that significant? Maybe.

I yawned and decided I should get ready to sleep. I brushed my teeth, and wiped down the sink, then returned to the bedroom, slipped under my burgundy covers and was out like a light.

A few hours later
CRACK

I twitched and sat up quickly. My shoulders tensed as I got up and ran towards the window. I stared out the window as it started to pour. *Water, not exactly Spence's favorite*, I thought.

I always seem to get on his nerves about that fact. He also hated the taste of water. I was always the person who made fun of him that he's the only person who cares about how water tastes. *Why am I thinking about Spence?*

Suddenly, I heard a loud crack and bright light filled the room. Everything turned into an unfamiliar darkness, not something that happens in May. There seemed to be an artificial green light coming from somewhere. Everything seemed cold and constrictive, and then I realized I was falling fast.

I could barely see a thing as I fell deeper, deeper, deeper into a murky, vast tunnel pushing me farther down. Then all of a sudden I felt my back collide with what seemed like dark, blood colored bricks that had lush green, blue, purple, and red grass around them. That's some strange grass I thought as I looked up at the sky. It was still pretty dark, but not as dark as it was when I was falling through the tunnel. The sky was a hazy, blue-purple with red clouds. *Where am I?*

"I think I broke my shoulder," someone muttered to the arid air that seemed to be weighing on me as I stood up. I wanted to collapse back down, but I forced myself back up. I recognized his black hair. *Spencer.*

"Get up," I ordered, then grabbed his wrist and pulled him up. I fingered over the black choker I wore every day. Engraved on the choker was the word water. I felt faint and weak. *Come on, Mia, that's not who you are. You aren't weak.* I still felt my skin become pale and cold.

"Water," Spence read from my choker.

"Yeah," I replied shortly.

"That's the same choker Elaine gave to you, right?" Spence asked.

"Yeah," I repeated. Elaine had given me the leather choker with the meaning for Maya when she tried to convince me to change my name.

I could see that Spence was rolling words around his mouth, obviously giving thought to whether or not he should say something to me. I wanted to tell him that he doesn't have to keep things from me. That I could keep a secret. *Did it have to do with Elaine?*

"Yeah," I repeated, but this time softer. I stopped myself from telling him that he doesn't have to keep secrets. Maybe I had been thinking wrong. Maybe he wasn't keeping something from me through all the years I had known him.

Deep breaths, Mia. I let go the breath I didn't realize I was holding and filled my lungs with air again, then slowly started breathing normally again. I felt my shoulders relax. *Easy does it, Mia.*

I gazed down because I didn't want to look him in the eye. I didn't want to know what he was thinking, or if he was hiding something from me. *Focus, Mia. Think about what the letters told you.* I sharply turned around. The scene made my face turn paler, but I couldn't look away. The realization that I hadn't fully admitted before became shockingly clear: This was the High Tide Challenge. Everything I had heard was true.

Chapter Four

Pineapples Don't Float

"We're in High Tide," I gasped.

"The letter we got from Nerissa was true," Spence said in awe. *That's right. He got Nerissa's letter too. He had told me all about it after I showed him my copy.*

Before we had time to take this all in, something got in our way. The "thing" was posed like a cat, ready to pounce any minute. Even crouching down low like it was doing the limbo, the animal was still taller than Spencer and me combined. I felt smaller than ever. Its eyes were a glittering red, filled with rage. Its fur was a shade of glistening gold, and it had some resemblance to a lion, except its tail was a hissing snake, the same color as its revolting eyes. The snake's pink tongue stuck out as it hissed.

There was a platform hovering on top of it. Stabbed into it were what seemed like millions of swords, daggers, and gadgets. There was a tall, frail rope ladder leading to the platform, blowing in the soft wind.

Answer three riddles and I shall let you pass, its voice hissed through my mind, uncomfortably. I covered my ears with my hands, yet I could still hear it. *What walks on four legs at dusk, two legs in the light, and three legs in the darkness?*

"A human," I said. The words spilled out of my mouth before I could control them.

Right. Next question, it snarled in my mind, baring its sharp, fang- like teeth. Its eyes flickered to a yellow color. The beast shivered, shook itself off, and then started to speak again. *I flicker. I flame. I'm light but not alive.*

"A candle."

I want to hear the boy now, Ms. Mia Lopez.

Hey, how does it know my name?

No eyes, but indeed saw. Thoughts before, but now empty. What is it?

I frowned, already knowing the answer. Spencer paused for a minute as if he was thinking. I knew he knew the answer. *You're not stupid, Spencer! Say it!*

"A skull."

No way! The red-eyed creature in front of us grimaced. Blue fire blew from its mouth. Far away from us it pounced. *Think fast, Mia.* I rubbed my choker and then I remembered the words in Nerissa's letter. *In High Tide you achieve small powers that won't work once you get back on Earth, so use them carefully.*

I need to climb that ladder! I scrambled to the ladder putting one brown combat boot on the first rope step, and then I did something I never thought I would do, ever. I climbed the ladder.

"Go quick," I managed to call to Spencer. "I'll be right behind you. I have an idea."

When he was halfway up the ladder, Spencer screamed.

"WHAT ARE YOU DOING?" The beast snarled at him. Spencer cringed away from it.

"You'll see!" I mouthed and I kept climbing. Up and up. The rope ladder was rocking back and forth because of my weight and the wind. It went sideways once and I grabbed on tighter in the opposite direction. The ladder couldn't carry my weight and started pulling apart. I frantically climbed higher. Finally, I got to the top.

"You're going to die up there!" Spencer muttered. I stepped up on one of the planks that made the platform as it wobbled under my feet from the tiring climb. I saw Spence was trying to kick the oversized monster.

"Hey, hey! Fluffy! Focus on me!" Spence called as the beast did a one hundred eighty degree head turn towards him. It blew fire. Yes, fire on him, but he appeared to be just fine. *How?*

Anyway, I needed to find my bravery and get this over with. Otherwise, Spencer might die and same with me. *Time to do this Mia. Your life depends on what you do right now, this second.* I took a slow breath in. I heard waves crashing from behind and looked behind me at the sea. The strong, salty smell of the sea became more pungent. *This better work.*

Spence found a moment to look at me. His eyes said, *You're probably the stupidest person in the world. Your ideas never work.* I bet Spence was thinking about that one time when I tried to make a whole pineapple float in a pool. Hence the word *tried,* but, hey, I was only seven. Spence had a point though. My ideas never work. They're probably the shallowest things in the world. I do whatever comes to mind first. I like to get things over with as soon as possible. Elaine was always bothering me about my stupidness when I don't think things through.

Focus, I thought in a rush. *Stop thinking about useless things that don't matter at the moment.*

I heard the beast growl loudly at Spence. I turned my head towards my best friend. Angrily, the beast attempted to swat Spence like a fly with its claw. Spencer punched it square on the nose. Its snake tail furiously slapped the ground and its pink tongue darted out of its mouth as it hissed. The animal prepared itself to pounce, but Spencer ducked underneath the creature and grabbed its furry leg before it had a chance to move.

*KA-BOOM! *

I coughed because smoke was rising towards me from the thick, red flames. *The creature blew blue blaze. Wait, where did the red come from?* My eyes watered because of gray smoke that was doubling in size by the minute. *Focus, Mia. Focus, focus, focus.* I turned my head back to the salty smell that came from the blue-green water. I sat down on the planks and reached my fingers towards the water. I heard the footsteps of someone walking on the wooden planks. Thud. Thud. *Focus.*

"What are you doing?!" a boy's voice started before I hastily shushed him. *There goes my focus.*

Spence ignored me and started babbling his know-it-all-mouth off again. "That's not going to work, Mia! Whatever you're doing," he retorted.

"Shush!" I screamed as something blue streaked from my shaking hand, eventually covering the beast below. The water drowned the hapless beast as it blew weak puffs of gray smoke. I coughed again, breathing in the last bit of smoke. The creature's eyes flicked back to yellow and then turned a bright, silvery white. I froze at the horrific sight. I wished I could look away, but I stayed put out of fear. *I can now kill easily with my bare hands. What else is new?* I shivered, not because it was chilly but because of my own thoughts.

Spence grinned. "That was brilliant," he shouted. I squeezed Spence's arm with a hint of a smile.

A minute later, just when we were both starting to relax, Spence's High Tide power came to light. I observed sparks jumping from one of his hands to his other, and he didn't even seem to notice. "Spence! Your hand is on fire and you're not burned whatsoever." I wasn't even trying to hide my fear. My instincts made me inch away to get far from the red sparks inside his fists that were turning into flames. More smoke was rising. Spence quickly balled his hands so that the fire would stop. He was clenching so tightly, his knuckles turned white. I shivered again and crossed my arms, feeling the beat of my heart through my arms. Thud, thud, thud, thud. A continuous, fast paced beat. *How long would it last?*

"You can create water, and I can create flames. I shouldn't be so surprised," Spence stated, looking me in the eye with his bright, green eyes. I rolled my eyes so that I wouldn't have to look in his. I stood up, and kicked a piece of wood from the platform.

"There is something under here," I clarified since my foot wasn't leveled, yanking a wood plank from the platform. Underneath was a little wooden box that held something silver. I didn't yet realize what it was. I kicked a piece of metal from below the wood. I kicked the metal up as Spence stared at it and yanked a sword from the planks of old wood. He spun the item in his hand as I caught the metal object. The circular object shined brightly in the light. *A shield.* The shield had a circular engraving of waves and broken pillars creating a border for the waves. I looked at the actual sea, and broken pillars like in the engraving surrounded the water. I took the chain made out of metal rings linked together that was attached to the shield and slung it over my head on to my shoulder.

"Come on, Spence. Let's get down," I murmured in a soft voice as I hopped on the swaying ladder. Spence watched me as I climbed down before he started to do so too.

"Has it occurred to you that we're probably going to die, Mia?" he asked after climbing down.

"You're not burned," I remarked randomly, not thinking about what I was saying. *As usual I can't stop myself from saying whatever is on my mind,* I scowled at myself.

Spence looked down at his clothing. He had on the same attire of jeans and a t-shirt that he always wore. Like how

I always wear my choker and my brown, fake leather combat boots. Spence finally realized he wasn't singed. "You can create water," he stated again as if that was a reason enough.

"And, no," I replied to Spence's earlier question. *Don't let him see you're scared, Mia. You're stronger than that. You're not a little girl anymore. You're an eleven-year-old, almost twelve, Mia. You aren't seven anymore.*

"We're not going to die! We're undoubtedly going to win. Mia Lopez and Spencer Campbell don't go down so easily." I pulled on my lying mask to speak with confidence. My breaths were strong and steady. I listened to the sound of myself sucking air in slowly then blowing out softly. *That's it. Easy does it. Nothing is going to pull me down, not today. I've got this. No one else will die.* I acted as though I wasn't perturbed by what might happen next. *Be brave Mia. Be brave.*

Chapter Five

Meet Me by the Sea

An Hour and Forty-five Minutes Later…

We started walking until something stopped me cold. The confidence I had before was gone and replaced with a dead, icy sweat. Hair stuck to my face. I tried to brush it off my pale face, but it was stuck like strong glue. Like super glue even. I held my breath as a whispering voice carried into my head. It started something like this:

She fights through to strive. Only for another to stay alive. But a final breath a boy must take. While the rest must ache.

"Spence? Did you hear that?" I cried. The air seemed to pulse out of me. It was like someone punched me with a boxing glove in the stomach. *There goes my lying mask. Where did your strength go, Mia? Get a hold on yourself and remember to breathe.* I took a cleansing breath in and let in out unhurriedly.

"Hear what?" Spence inquired. *Was I going insane? Why couldn't Spence hear the voices?*

"A voice. Near the sea." My voice was getting smaller by the second. *In and out, Mia. Deep breaths. You aren't insane.*

"The Call of Marissa. The person most in danger hears it," Spence said so softly it seemed as if he was talking to himself. Good, I really wasn't insane or crazy. Or anything of the sort.

"How did you—?" I scrunched up my eyebrows. *How is he so smart?*

"I did some research." *Of course he did. He's Spence.*

After all I had felt, this was worse. Way worse. Worse than my mom dying. The feeling of fear crept through my body. The feeling was unbridled, making me shake in my shoes. I had never felt this way and I felt helpless. I felt vulnerable and controlled, but I let it happen anyway. My knees buckled down and the world's weight crashed down beside me. I felt my knees scrape against the hard, blood red bricks. The lights dimmed. Then they went out. They were replaced with a voice. The female voice didn't even bother to sound nice.

Meet me near the sea. You'll be grateful.

Lightly my vision fluttered. Everything was blurred and I could hear Spence's voice along with waves crashing. It all seemed so far away, but so close. *Mia, you need to get up.* I wobbled to a sitting position. The cold sweat wouldn't go away. My hands quivered. All I could smell was thick smoke, even though the fire from the creature I had killed was far away. I coughed. The air was almost choking me. I tried to take a deep breath, but instead of blowing the air out easily I coughed.

"How long was I out?" I interrogated, sitting on the ground after clearing my throat.

"An hour, Mia. What happened?" Spence questioned, worry hidden in his voice.

"An hour," I echoed, not answering his query. I stood up, thoughts rushing to my brain. Spence stayed behind me, but gave me room. It was almost like he could read minds. I was grateful for that. I stuffed my hands in my black legging pockets.

I felt something hugging me. My vision blurred again until all I could see was a terrible, shocking crimson. After that the world went faster than the speed of lighting. All things tightened up and seemed claustrophobic. It almost was as if there was a boa constrictor on me, about to swallow its prey.

I realized I still had my shield in my hand. I held it near my face. Over the piece of armor, my eyes watched the view of the High Tide Sea and the rock I assumed Marissa used to sit on. My trap closed up with what seemed to be vines, just like the ones on roses.

Chapter Six

I Didn't Care About Plants until Now

I heard the sound of metal against the bricks. The dusty rose colored vines' grip tightened around my wrists and they started turning a blueish green. The thorny vines grew tighter across my shield, making it uncomfortable to hold on to it. I could feel the pricks dig into my skin. The vines pushed my hands to my chest tightly. I still held onto the shield the best that I could, but the plant forced me to the ground, burying me halfway in the dirt, grass, and bricks. Hoping that it might do something to help, I let my water, something that now felt normal, drown the plants. The tiny thorns cut a gash into my face.

SCRATCH!

Oh my gosh, Spence! I felt the plant let loose and fall down against my eye. The pricks pierced against it. Now, all I could see was red. It hurt so badly.

"Ow!" I cried when my eye got hit.

Burning pain shot through my face as I rose to my feet. I brushed some of the dirt off me. I could taste the dry grime in my mouth and the salty smell of blood-my blood-dripping from my eye. To my surprise, something remarkable happened. I felt a pulsing sensation against my skin. I touched my cut once and dropped my right arm to my side. I expected blood to start gushing out of my eye and from the cut below where I put pressure on, but instead I felt my skin stretching. I blinked a couple of times and the red I was seeing was gone. Even though I knew the cut was gone, because I was not seeing red anymore, I could feel the burning feeling from my eye all the way down to my cheek.

We were both speechless, because of the abnormality here. Even though the bleeding stopped, my face was still throbbing, from my eye down to my cheek. "We need to get out of here quickly," I muttered. Spence nodded his head in agreement.

I dusted off my shield, throwing the silver chain attached to it over my head again. I kicked Spence's weapon that was buried under the muddy bricks, letting the grime fly up in the process. Spence caught the sword.

I paced back and forth, ready to go any second. I queried swiftly to Spence, "You coming?"

Spence looked behind his shoulder, subtly, as if there was an answer there. Then he answered quietly, "Yeah, I am."

I slightly smiled while Spence followed me, as if one of us knew where we were going. As if we knew what was going to happen next. But, I guess, we can't know everything.

Chapter Seven

I'm Not Here for You

A slight breeze blew an object towards me and I caught it. It landed softly on my palm, almost as if it was meant to be there. I listened to the crunch of the paper as my fingers folded over the note. In smooth, gold writing were the haunting words I had first heard what seemed like weeks ago, *Meet me near the sea. You'll be grateful.*

***

I pulled out the piece of parchment in my pocket, reading the work for about the hundredth time. It was the only thing that stuck with me. The thing that needed me to react. No, I'm not talking about the letter I had received from my mother. That letter seemed far away, distant, like I received it years ago. The note that I recently got forced me to follow. I felt a great need to do what it said—*I can't believe I'm going to do this.*

I inched away from Spence as far as possible, my head denying every thought of why I shouldn't do this. *I need to do this, I have to.* I just wished I could tell him what I was about to do, what I was going to do, but the letter specifically said to not tell anyone.

1—2—3—My mind raced, wondering what was going to happen and if it would work. And then:

CRACK!

I vanished away from Spence. I teleported.

The next thing I knew, I was stepping on a glossy, arched bridge that had aged cracks throughout.

CRACK!

The second time I heard that sound I felt my feet hit the water, stinging.

A muffled voice from above the water spoke, although I couldn't make out the words. A delicate but strong hand pulled me. I could feel the water trying to push me down, giving me a headache. The hand came from a pale, blond-haired girl. Her hair had perfect beach waves. She wore a crossover, gray top and blue, ripped denim.

"Welcome Mia," the girl invited. Her voice trying to be pleasant, but her face showed otherwise.

The girl's bubble gum, pink eyes turned more into a strawberry color that studied each part of me. "Maybelle," the girl articulated, sticking her hand out. I let my eyes linger on the sight of her hand until Maybelle dropped it and said, "Looks like someone is sassy."

Maybelle laughed as she spoke without humor in her tone. *Maybelle. Where have I heard that name before?* A jolt of remembrance hit me. *The letter: The two friends' names were Marissa and Maybelle. Marissa is known for her half bald, bright blue and green hair, while Maybelle is known for her temper.*

My eyes flicked towards an aimlessly hanging bubble above the rock I was standing on. The bubble was clear, but wisps of smoke filled the inside. I caught sight of a tiny girl, her blue hair in her face. Her head was leaning against the bubble she was resting in, as if she was knocked out cold. Maybe she was. I shivered. *This place is dangerous. I need to be careful like my English teacher, Mrs. Young, said.*

"I'm not here for you," I said, clearing the air after a long moment of silence, my eyes falling back to hers.

"You're here for your mom. Your mom died a while ago. Nice to meet you personally again, Mia. I'm Nerissa," a girl with a black, short bob with red highlights added. A sudden flashback of the letter appeared again. Then I remembered the English teacher had told me to *be careful.* I realized who she was—my English teacher. *Yours truly, Nerissa.* The story is true. I stumbled to my feet. Suddenly, I didn't feel like myself. *Who are these people? What do they want from me? And most importantly, Why am I here and not someone else?*

Chapter Eight

Mia

"They'll be High Tide Police," Maybelle warned. I thought of Maybelle's fair exchange. She had told me that if I work for her I'd get what I really want.

"Lots of them," Nerissa threw in. Nerissa's words proved that she was the same person who wrote the flowy words of the letter that laid in the closet of Elaine's house. I stared at Nerissa's clear eyes. A twinge of sorrow fell on her face, or so I thought. I'm not as good at reading people as Spencer is.

"Wait—what police?" I wondered out loud.

"The High Tide Police," Maybelle said. "They have the ability to teleport, meaning they can easily send children down to High Tide, the best underground world in the nation!" she slowly said as if I couldn't understand.

"The *only* underground world of the nation," Nerissa sighed as if she corrected Maybelle a lot. Maybelle put her hand up as a sign of peace and to stop fighting.

Maybelle sucked in a slow breath through clenched teeth. "Anyway, stay away from the police and find the Trap to make sure nobody escapes from it," she warned.

My mom's letter. Elliot almost escaped from it. "The what?" I asked to make sure.

"The Trap. Only thing that's somewhat easier to break out from than the rest of the High Tide doors. We locked the other doors in a special way so they can't get out. Otherwise, the High Tide Challenge would be over and we'd lose." *She is able to lose. We all can. Life really is a game.*

I grimaced. "So that's why I'm still here?"

Maybelle's eyes turned a shade of maroon. "Without being trapped here, you wouldn't have the chance of bringing your mom back."

"What happens if when the High Tide Challenge is over you haven't escaped?"

Maybelle answered in a monotone voice. "You'd probably burn because of the bomb that lights yearly to represent the new Queen or the present Queen who would keep her position. It all depends on where the bomb is placed."

Maybelle had said this with no fervor. "Also, the High Tide Challenge stops you from being hungry and heals your cuts, but when the challenge is over you are no longer protected. So, likely, if you escape from being blow up, you'd die of hunger or thirst, or some sort of disease."

Before getting up from my sitting position in the secret room which lied inside the rock, I swirled my pointer finger at Maybelle, but then switched the direction and pointed my finger at the newly built bridge after the old one collapsed. Green and blue whirls of vines grew against it, making it look more vintage-looking. *I have more than one power. I am a Neutral.* Maybelle had explained what a Neutral was in her note. She said it happened to all heirs of Marissa. Since Marissa was related to all the Queens and one Tech (the people who generate High Tide), she, like all Neutrals is able to have more than one strength. Most of them seemed to like one power better than the rest of them and use that more often. Mine was water, just like Nerissa's.

Maybelle's eyes turned a shade of gray with a shade of hazel that matched her new shirt. "Yes, lastly remember—"

"Yes, I remember. No need to remind me. Just don't," I sighed, sounding like Nerissa. *I didn't want to do this.*

"Now, shoo Lopez," Maybelle instructed. I didn't need to be ordered twice. I turned on my heels and started walking, but her soft voice stopped me. "You're a Neutral. You are strong. Nothing can get in your way, Mia. Remember that."

I turned towards her, but my lips were shut together. *That's right, Mia. Nothing can get in your way. You are strong. You can do anything. You—you are a Neutral.*

Chapter Nine

You Have To Know That I Didn't Actually Want To Do This

*C*heck our surroundings, Mia. Make sure there is no one *around besides Spence.* I turned my head a different direction. My hair whipped in my face after I had teleported back to the place I had left Spence. *This is something I have to get used to.* I blew a piece of my dark, curly hair back. My eyes flicked back and forth. *No one's watching. Good.* I made the mistake of staring at Spence for a quick millisecond, so I instantly looked away. *I can't even look at him anymore because of how I abruptly left him.*

Fire burned on one of my hands and water soaked the other. Spence's face was like, *How? That's right. He doesn't know I am a Neutral.*

"Your choice," I said gruffly. The old, faded scar I had by my jawline wasn't covered by my hair like it normally is. So, I quickly covered it with my curls. I made sure my eyes were looking down like there was something interesting on the ground. I didn't want to look at my best friend.

"Why are you doing this?" Spence half screamed.

"It—it wasn't my choice. Now choose one, fire or water." I was surprisingly calmer as I stuttered my answer.

"Fire," Spence responded. I put one of my hands down. The water disappeared.

I took my blazing hand and the fire grew and I disappeared. I hid by the forest nearby as the dirt ground split in two, allowing chunks of dirt and rubble to slip through—and Spence dropped in the cut. The earth fixed itself again. *Breathe, Mia. Spencer will be fine. You did the right thing, to give him the chance to escape.*

I couldn't believe I did that. I totally did the opposite of what Maybelle wanted me to do. I wondered what Maybelle was going to do with me. *At least Spencer has probably escaped by now from the Trap. At least he doesn't have to deal with this torturous place anymore.* I let go a breath, shaking. *What if Spencer isn't smart enough to escape the Trap and he's still stuck in the darkness of the hole?* I shook my head at the thought, *No, this is Spencer we're talking about.*

I walked towards the bridge to face my fears of talking to Maybelle, but then I heard voices.

"Why are you doing this?!" a hysterical voice asked. *No doubt, that's Nerissa's high voice.* "Why? Because you're jealous? Because you want to be them? Because you want to be as powerful as them? Or is it just because you don't want to be overthrown from your position of being a Queen?" Maybelle growled, but didn't dare speak.

Nerissa's eyes got glassy. "You used to be one of them before. You know how it feels to be pressured, how vicious this world is, and how hard it is to stay alive. You're making it worse." Nerissa started shaking, her hands quivering like crazy. She was also blinking insanely to push the tears back.

"I couldn't care less!" Maybelle's scream shocked me. It ran out farther than the chipped off, broken pillars that stood feet away from her. It seemed to creep into my body and shatter my bones. Her voice was something to be afraid of, but I stayed calmer than before. I leaned behind the pillar. The broken pillar was only like a foot taller than me. I held my breath so Maybelle wouldn't hear me. "I'm not them anymore. I can do whatever I want now, right? Right now, the problem is Spencer. He is one of the last High Tide kids left, isn't he? And he's alive!"

"It doesn't matter, May-May. The boy's fated to die anyway. You know it and so do I," Nerissa griped. *May-May. A nickname for Maybelle. It almost seems as if they were friends before.*

"That's not my name, and it needs to happen faster. We're running out of time." *Time. The only topic Maybelle seems fascinated by these days.*

"Maybelle, whatever. Leave him alone. Deal with something else."

"Change your tone, Nerissa. You should be praising me for letting you be under my care!"

"Right. Like I needed to be," Nerissa deadpanned.

Maybelle's glare seemed to burn the entire sea that they were in the middle of. "I only ask you to do one thing! And *you still haven't gotten to work.*"

"I *will,* May-May."

"That's not my name," Maybelle irked, "and *Spencer* is still alive. It's not a good thing." A rush of shock rushed through me after hearing his name. Keen to hear more, I listened more carefully.

"I know he is and he might as well stay that way." Nerissa's eyes flickered to Marissa, the hapless girl who was still in Maybelle's trap. If Maybelle felt guilty, she didn't show it. Her face was more still than a stone. I know that she noticed she had done wrong because her eyes started with a shade of dark red, then turned a salmon color to prove my point.

Nerissa's eyes flew back to Maybelle. She had dyed streaks of her black, short bob with red accents. She wore tight blue jeans that had cuts, and a matching denim jacket along with it.

The two bickering women didn't realize I was watching them the entire time. I stepped on the bridge that led to the island-looking rock. I started a small flick of flame on my finger. I shivered in surprise at what I had done. *What am I doing?* Fire burned Maybelle's house down. Flame was a fear I've grown to share with them.

Their names were Addy and Adaline and in the process they lit Maybelle's house on fire, causing her mother to die. The vision of reading the letter flashed through my mind again. At least the accident was actually an accident. Addy and Adaline didn't mean to start the fire. They tried to kill Marissa and flee the scene. Maybelle wasn't there when the fire was lit. I could have stopped the fire that killed *my* mother. I could have stopped the person who started the fire, but I was too young and dumb.

My eyes burned with salty water and I thought, *Don't cry.* But, of course, the tears fell down anyway.

Chapter Ten

To Be Understood
is to Understand

The feel of cool rocks and sand pushing against my toes with the flow of the sea was very pleasant.

The idea that I just threw up, however, was not.

My socks that were stuffed sloppily in the small opening of my boots and the shield I received rested on the dry part of the sand as I took in the salt smell from the water. The sea was a green-blue, each wave its own unique shade. I stepped deeper into the cold water, shivering a bit. I let the tips of my fingers glide against the motion of the water. I blinked and looked back at where Maybelle was. She had her infamous annoyed bottom lip pout fixed on her face as she shifted her weight between her feet often. The tips of her thin, blonde hair looked damp and wavy. I trotted against the water to reach for my shield and boots. I slung the nylon shield strap beside my neck and positioned the shield across my body. I grabbed both shoes with one hand, pressing my feet onto the hard rocks into the sand, leaving little dents in my skin. I tip-toed barefoot, feeling an aching pain on my feet from the rocks stuck to the top layer of my skin, towards the wooden bridge. The dry bridge soaked in water from my feet. The cool, damp wind was stronger on the bridge and blew everyone's hair westward. The hairs on my arms stood up as I walked down the bridge.

Nerissa was obviously annoyed with Maybelle and was sitting on the ground at the end of the bridge, slouched over. She glared at Maybelle by squinting her already narrow eyes. Her hair blew in front of her, but she didn't bother to pull it back. Her chin was hidden as it rested against her bare arms. Resting above her arm, her thin lips were a dark shade of natural pink. Even with the moisture from the air, her lips were dry and slightly cracked. Flushing from the cold, Nerissa's cheeks were as pigmented as her lips. Nerissa seemed to purposely not notice me, keeping her fixed glare at Maybelle.

Maybelle, on the other hand, noticed me immediately. Her lips curled up, but she certainly wasn't smiling. She lifted her thin fingers to my hair in an attempt to give me an affectionate, loving rub on the head, but her coarse, dry hands were not gentle and accidentally pushed me forward, knocking my boots onto the bridge. I took that as an opportunity to reach for my socks to start to get my shoes on. Maybelle snorted, resting her back against the railing of the bridge, as I tried to shove my wet feet into my black, narrow socks.

Maybelle tried her best to smile and opened her mouth to speak. "I need a favor." Maybelle walked forward as I worked on hopping towards her while failing at tying my shoes while walking. Maybelle pointed to a silver, metal building. Behind the building was a luscious array of tropical trees. The sky over in the area looked like a darker shade of purple with low-lying, ashy gray fog to replace the red ones that hung above us. The Tech building didn't look far, maybe only a couple of feet, but it almost looked like a whole other world. "That's the Tech building. They help create everything that's here," Maybelle said, then looked at me and reached over to pat my head. I moved to my left to move away from her hand. She glared at me but it wasn't condescendingly. *That's a first.*

Maybelle let out a nasally breath as a replacement for a laugh. "I know you're going to be curious." Maybelle's face then darkened. "But, you will only go in, grab the Search Box from Lauren Parker, and come *straight back.* Understood?" Maybelle extended her last word.

I nodded. "Understood."

Maybelle huffed as if she was stressed. She was showing self-comforting methods; her fingers wrapped around thin arms to hug herself.

"I'm trusting you, okay, Mia?"

See, *trust* was an unusual word. The word is usually thought of as something appointed by those who have gotten to know you but is often tossed around with people who are close to strangers. Teachers *trust* you to do your assignments. Your hairdresser *trusts* you to give them a tip. But the type of trust Maybelle gave me was very unusual. There was no guarantee that I was going to be of any help to her, and she doesn't know me well, but Maybelle took a leap of faith for someone as simple as me. It almost felt validating that I was finally given a chance in the first place. It was freeing. And that was the problem. That was what sucked me into Maybelle's plan in the first place. It wasn't fear of Maybelle and, surprisingly, it wasn't hope either. It was our strange sense of *similarity.*

A random sound of water splashing the bridge unsettled Maybelle and she dug her nails into my shoulder. I glared at her hand and pulled my shoulder away as I saw Maybelle subtly look at Marissa's aura mass.

And that's when I got it. I completely understood Maybelle Monel. Heck, I could sum her up in one word: *jealously.* When Marissa was praised for her bravery and perseverance,

Maybelle was left with a burned home and no one left. The respect she never had before was definitely not filled with her dominance over Nerissa. So, all that was left was her anger towards both of them.

At least it didn't happen in front of her. At least she had no input. She had no way to stop it. I couldn't say the same.

I continued to walk on the dark red brick trail that guided me towards the Tech building. The trail had fewer bricks and more of the dense, soft adhesive that cushioned my walk. Dull, silver murkiness swarmed around me, making it hard to see the metal structure of the Tech Building.

Unfortunately, the walk gave me time to think about Maybelle and the memory of my mom. It left a hollow feeling in my chest as I felt my eyes burn red. My eyes threatened tears as I tried to blink them back.

But, of course, they fell down anyway.

Chapter Eleven

Lost is Subjective

It wasn't that the lady was tall or large. Her presence was just strong.

I pressed my back against the rough bark of a tree next to me. I could feel the coarseness of the bark stick to my clothing. Worried about making noise, I tried not to move. Without moving my body, I shifted my neck so I could see behind me.

The woman's platforms made a thumping sound as she walked across the brick path. She wore all cream-colored clothes beside her black zip-up and her matching shoes. Her tank top's thin strips fell neatly on her shoulders. Its back was on the lower side and dropped perfectly against the curve of her back. Her matching satin-like skirt wasn't attached. One side hung lower than the other and the ruffles towards the bottom fell right under her knees. She slung one of the sleeves of her sweater over the tank top on her left side, and the other side was placed near her elbows. I could tell the sweater was a zip-up by the plastic zig-zag cut out on her right, although I couldn't see the zipper since only her right side was facing towards me. Hearts with little angry faces on her sweater stared at me. Her shoes had the same pattern. Little plastic hearts were attached to the black laces as well.

The woman huffed at something and smiled, her left side

reaching higher than her right. She didn't show her teeth when she smiled, her top-heavy lips pressed down together. Her nose was on the flatter side and it burned a shade of red as if she had a cold. Her hair was cut short, almost shaved completely off. By the texture of it, it seemed dense. The short coils in her hair reminded me of mine. I looked up to one of my coils of hair sticking to my face. I blew on it, trying to get it to move without exposing myself. Maybe I needed to cut my hair too.

I hugged myself closer so I couldn't be seen at all. I extended my neck to see the woman better. She had an odd fieriness to her. There was a peachiness to the darkness of her skin. She radiated a sense of brightness. She reminded me of pale green vines, the ones that hang from buildings, although it looked like she could burn them up in seconds.

There was no possibility that she didn't have the fire manipulation ability. And so I concluded that she had to be Queen Allison, the one Queen I hadn't met yet.

Another presence distracted me. He seemed to be there before, but I didn't see him. How could I miss such a familiar face? His face was washed out of color, but his cheeks flushed red. His dark copperish black hair fell down to the cheekbones of his heart-shaped face. A couple of light freckles dusted the sides of his nose. The guy, who I spent a little less than half my life with, seemed odd to come across. I was always aware of how different we were, yet it never occurred to me that we might take different sides of a situation. I always thought he had my back, but maybe I was the one who didn't have his. I was reminded of the first day of High Tide when I realized how secretive Spencer was being. Spence was never an open or vocal person, opting out of speaking in class and keeping his sentences "concise" as he liked to call it, but this was something entirely different. I tell him everything and he listens, so did he think that

I wouldn't listen to him? Part of me wanted to blame it on his introvertedness, but he never was that way to me. It was his choice to check up on me each day so I would not be alone, although I always found that strange.

Yet every time he visited my house, he wasn't worried about me. It was as if he was concerned about Elaine, my house, or what would get the both of us in trouble. The idea unsettled me.

But now that I was here, worrying about Elaine and her relationship with Spencer did me no good. I was more worried about Spencer escaping, but of course he was stubborn towards the idea. The fact that he didn't listen to me made my blood boil. I hated not being respected and I hated that he thought he was smarter than me. He annoyed me.

Spencer turned his head left towards the currently unknown woman, "You have to be Allison." *Of course he thought that too. He probably came to that conclusion before me.*

The left corner of Allison's mouth shifted upwards and she ever so slightly lifted her eyebrows. She paused, her posture moderately moved forward before she opened her mouth. "Queen," she paused again, probably for effect. "Allison. Queen of the Sun."

I snorted softly to myself. It was ironic she was called the Queen of the Sun since there was no sun in High Tide. The sky had some natural elements of light that slightly brightened the area around us. She was the Queen of fire. Of heat. She embodied the ability to manipulate fire. Just like the ability Spencer had.

"You're supposed to be missing." Spence pressed his eyebrows together in confusion. He was right. Maybelle had always told me she didn't know where she was.

Allison smiled, huffed air from her nose, closed her eyes for a few seconds, and opened her mouth. "That information is from Maybelle. You see, what she doesn't understand is that I am very fond of my individuality. That means I don't like how she controls my position as Queen. And I am very fond of my position." Allison lowered her eyes down at Spencer. "You've been showing other competitors the Trap, so it's not hard to assume you want them gone so you can take *my* position."

Other competitors? I had always assumed that there were more people here because of Maybelle's frantic urge to block all the exits, and the idea that there could be a descendant taking the place of each current Queen at the end of the challenge, but I hadn't thought much of it.

There was no doubt in my mind that Maybelle would be provoked if someone escaped for the first time. Allison said that Spencer was sending other competitors to one of High Tide's exits, the Trap. I huffed, recalling the letter I was given by my mom. My grandfather was found outside that exit. Could there be an obstacle there too? Is that why no one was able to escape?

But the thing that unsettled me the most was Spencer's motives while trying to lead competitors out. I was pretty certain no one had escaped yet, so was Spencer leading them there purposefully or was he trying to help without knowing the dangers? How did he get into contact with the other competitors?

Spencer knit his eyebrows closer together, placing his hands in his pockets. The knees of his gray cargo pants were soiled with dirt and so were his tennis shoes. His black long-sleeved shirt didn't reveal any marks, but its once neatly ironed appearance was gone. The top part of his shirt mostly remained untouched but the ends of his shirt were creased in all directions. His sleeves were rolled up past his elbows. A line of dried mud was caked into his left arm. It was a strange visual coming from a guy who valued cleanliness.

Spencer opened his mouth slightly. "They weren't able to

escape?" It wasn't said remorsefully but rather in a curious fashion.

He used the competitors to test out the dangers of the Trap so he didn't have to go himself. I gritted my teeth. I had to admit I didn't enjoy working with Maybelle and the line for my morals had been blurred with Maybelle's. But I knew this was wrong.

How could Spencer do this?

Allison bared her teeth this time when she smiled. "No." Her voice was softer, in a more matter-of-fact tone, but it kept the same bitterness to it. She pressed her lips together before speaking again. "And that's why I have to do this. Just in case the Trap doesn't do what it's supposed to do." She curled each finger into her palm and then thrust her pointer finger behind her.

I tried to recall my mom's letter about Elliot. Something was guarding the exit in the Trap to make sure no one could escape. All other possible exits were blocked off by Maybelle.

But Allison said that it was possible for the Trap to not work properly. I was curious to know what was in that area.

I tried to turn where Allison pointed but I couldn't see anything. I turned, placing my hand on the rough bark of the tree. Allison's sweater caught on fire from the seeping fire that burned from her nails. Her nail beds blared a bright crimson color as her cuticles burned.

I shuddered. The soft features of my mom's face flashed in my mind. I blinked my imagination back.

A smile line near Alison's Cupid's bow formed as she pushed the right side of her lips up and shrugged. She slowly let go of her hand that pointed behind her as her nails on that hand sparked flames. Allison gave a pity smile towards Spencer as she vanished in her own flame, leaving small yellow sparks behind. In her place came a beautiful animal. A beautiful yet stunningly unnerving monster. Its long, hooked fingernails sunk into the blood-red tiles below it. The bricks around it pushed up because of its force. Its scaly knees met the top of Spencer's face. *Oh. My. God.*

Chapter Twelve

The Rebirth of Spencer

Allison was like a freshly drawn bath. There was a sense of tranquility from the refreshing flow of water, but the bath rendered a little too hot to be comfortable. It felt good to scoop up the water and run it through your scalp, but your feet tingled as they squirmed under the depths of the hot water.

Allison was new and sincerely unique, but she was dangerous and I didn't want to feel the pain of my feet burning as the water started to fill up the tub.

But Allison wasn't my priority at the moment. I pressed my hands against the hard bark of the tree behind me. I was curious to see what Spencer would do next.

Fire instantly burned through his skin. I yelped as quietly as I could. *There is nothing to be afraid of, Mia, the fire wouldn't hurt you.*

I shivered at the idea that although the fire wouldn't physically harm me, I'd still be able to feel the burn from it.

I didn't want to think about burning alive. Especially not Spencer being the one to inflict that pain.

I chewed on my lip. It wasn't just Spencer who held such power. As a Neutral, I could, just as easily, burn someone in a few quick seconds.

I craned my neck to look at Spencer.

Despite the buzzing fear that hummed in my stomach, Spencer was a sight to see. His fire danced on his skin, jumping from the tips of his fingers to his biceps. He extended his arm forward to spark a brighter flame in his hand. The fire shone a light on his skin so that the areas that were exposed to the most luminosity made his skin look as if it was a translucent red. He glowed under the heat of his own flame.

Spencer stood silently, prepared to attack if the monster came forward. His eyes darted around in a desperate attempt to figure out a plan.

The light from his fire burned my eyes, but I couldn't take my eyes off of Spencer. Spencer's hair shone despite its usual dark appearance. He looked warm and lively.

With one sweep of his arm, Spencer created a flame wall between himself and the winged animal. Blue, red, and purple scales seemed to flash through the fire. The beast's skin could almost camouflage with the rest of High Tide. Grass, sky, bricks, and all. Spence ducked, knowing what was going to happen. The monster blew out a wellspring of water. Tucked in its back were baby blue wings. When they emerged, the monster seemed twice its actual size. Spence forced himself to stare at the dragon's purple eyes. Its mucky, gray fangs stuck out. All the colors and the shape of the dragon-like monster almost made the creature beautiful. The wings of the creature almost seemed angelic and free. I admired the features of the monster that the Techs had made.

No time to think of that now, Mia.

Spencer continued his gaze at the monster. I glared at the monster. How can this even exist? It almost looked like each scale on the monster changed a different color of blue in a way that made the scales look like they were moving even when the dragon was completely still. The dragon lowered its head, seemingly sniffing at Spencer to see if he was still alive.

I shifted my hand that was pressed against the oak tree next to me. The print of the bark stayed etched on my palm.

The opposite of water is fire. Could that help Spencer? But why did I even want to save Spencer? I grimaced at the thought of our last conversation. It didn't help when I recalled his secretive look when we entered High Tide. But he was still good old familiar Spencer and I liked familiar things.

I groaned as I rubbed my cold hands together. I certainly did not want to see fire again, nor have it burn against my hand. I looked at my hand and then at Spencer. I blew on my hand to spark the tiny flame on my fingers while I treaded towards Spencer's back. I rested my fiery hand on his shoulder as warmth crept back into his skin.

The hairs on the back of my neck stood up uncomfortably from the tingling feeling of air being blown onto my skin. My fingers curled in next to my palms as a reflex. My clenched fists turned my knuckles a shade close to white. I whipped my body towards the dragon who abruptly lifted its head to stop sniffing me. The dragon widened its eyes almost to make it look like it was pouting. I glared at the creature, my fists still in a fighting position. The dragon slowly opened its mouth. It looked like there was a gland on the top of its mouth that dripped down water. The same water it spewed at Spencer. As a result, I tried to control my shaky hands to make water swirl around my fingers. The glow of blue from my hands appeared to upset the creature as it closed its mouth while making an armpfh sound. It hung its head in a way that most of its long neck was still upright as it disintegrated. Particles of the dragon fell on my fists as I blinked the dust away from my eyes.

I furrowed my eyebrows. *Am I that scary?*

I never wanted to cover my sense of fear and pain in a way that Maybelle does. In a way that is so vile and inflicts her own pain onto others. But, in High Tide, my arrogance to protect my emotions have continuously backfired. I mean, that dragon was completely traumatized by me and I was the beast instead of it.

I let out a shaky breath as I dropped my arms. I unclenched my fists and stared at the dust falling down on the bricks making a small pile on the grass.

I placed my thumb on a bump on my chin from a small scar. I pushed the skin on my chin down as I rubbed the scar. Without moving my finger, I turned towards Spencer. Each time he breathed out I could see a cloud of air escaping from his lips. His dry lips were partially open as he took in another laborious breath. His right hand gripped his ribs as he leaned forward to balance himself using his left hand.

You helped him twice and the first time he didn't even listen to you. You don't need to help him again.

I looked over at the metal Tech Building. Reaching there was my priority at the moment, not helping Spencer. I needed to do this for Maybelle. I felt the pressure of wind push against me.

I looked back as Spencer looked away from me.

Chapter Thirteen

Orpheus and Eurydice

I t smelled distinctly of copper. The smell ran up my nose and made me gag.

"Look out!" a girl shrieked. I froze up as her hands reached my shoulders. Her cold fingers made adrenaline pump through my veins.

I looked up. A mass of black fur blocked my view. The creature was huge with four paws that were the size of my leg alone. My neck hurt looking up at it. Sharp canines reached the creature's chin. Or well…chins.

The animal had three heads. Three dog heads to be exact.

The three-headed dog's smell that accompanied the copper scent wasn't pleasant. It reeked of mud-soaked hair.

The girl scolded me, "What are you doing?" The girl stood in front of me, blocking the dog away from us with a wall of fire. My breath hitched as I stepped back.

She's like Spencer. Fire abilities.

"What can you do?" Her voice was loud and commanding.

The thoughts in my mind blurred. "Huh?" I questioned.

"You know, I can create fire, so what can you do?"

I turned around, noticing the trees near the Tech building. I had never used my plant manipulation abilities, but Maybelle said they existed.

A prickling feeling shot through my arm as the bark of

the trees created a shelter around us.

The girl beside me continued to clutch my shoulders as she shivered.

I furrowed my eyebrows. *A three-headed dog.* "This is a Greek mythology creature. Isn't he Cerberus?"

"You can't seriously be thinking about this now."

"No, no, no. Hear me out." I took a deep breath in as I heard the dog sniff around the bark sculpture around us. I spoke quieter, in hopes of not attracting the creature. "If these creatures are based on mythological stories, then their weaknesses would be too."

The girl nodded. "So, what are Cerberus's weaknesses?"

Remembering things was not my strong suit. "That man, in that one story, had that instrument that put it to sleep." I winced at my words. I sounded so stupid, but I could not remember the name of the story for the life of me.

"Orpheus and his lyre," the girl recognized. "We need to play music to put it to sleep and then kill it after."

I pointed to her. "How do we get music?"

"My friend. She came here with me. She brought one of those MP3 players."

"I could have brought stuff with me?" I whispered, a little too loudly.

The girl hushed me before speaking. "She brought whatever was in her pockets." The girl reached into my legging pocket. In her hands, she pulled out my school ID. My hair was all messy and I looked angry to have my photo taken. She laughed quietly, "You look great in this," she said as she put my ID in her own pocket.

"Hey! I might need that!" I exclaimed as loudly as I could while still whispering.

She laughed and raised her eyebrows. "No, I don't think you will."

I looked behind me into the darkness. "Any moment

now, Cerberus." As if on cue, Cerberus had chewed his way completely at the bark. "Run," I muttered at the girl.

The girl snatched my hand and guided me to where her friend was.

Her friend had no head. She was a limped body in a wheelchair, with no head. Dried blood crusted on her chest, from the flowed blood that once oozed out of her neck.

My legs felt shaky. I didn't want to stand anymore.

"Your friend is dead," I murmured.

"Yes, that's why I'm very much focused on keeping us alive," the girl grumbled as she reached into her friend's jean pockets.

I could hear in her voice that she'd seen death before. She had gotten used to these kinds of situations, but what shocked me was that she was so indifferent about her friend's death.

I wondered if I'd be that emotionless if Spencer died.

"Look out!" I screamed as Cerberus leaned down. I shook my hand. No fire. Of course, my abilities weren't working. *God.*

The girl collapsed on me, gliding an MP3 player into my hand.

My hand froze up. It came into contact with a liquid with a high viscosity.

The liquid was red.

I sucked my breath in as I fumbled with the MP3 player's power button.

The music device immediately started to play a piano instrumental.

Each of the three heads of the dog seemed fascinated by the music as their eyes started to grow dark. Its legs were neatly folded under each other as it laid its heads to rest.

I pushed the girl off me and gently onto the ground. Part of her torso had been bit off, but High Tide had already healed it.

"The pain is too bad; you have to fix it," she spat out.

Fix it?

"Where are you from? How many more High Tide Competitors are left? Are you okay?" I inquired, frantically.

"Do you really need to know all this? I am in extreme pain right now and-."

I interrupted her with my sudden realization, "No one's going to remember you here. Everyone you knew here is dead. They might remember you on Earth, but this world is different. They brought you here and they're not going to care that you died here." I paused to let in a strained breath. "How will I be able to look back and say that I knew you," I ruminated.

She looked at me dumbfounded, but then came to her senses as she scoffed, "I hate this stupid place. Fine. First of all, I'm not okay. I got bitten by that rabid thing." She paused, huffed, and then continued. "The two of us are from Maine. We're the last ones. We were looking for you, actually. We were trying to see how many of us are left." She inhaled shakily. "They all died near the Trap."

So Allison was right, Spencer was leading the other competitors to the Trap.

"Did you meet Spencer yet?"

"No, but I met one of the competitors and he spoke very highly of him. They said he was smart," she spluttered.

I wasn't surprised that Spencer was able to get people to love him. I mean, who wouldn't think highly of someone who was promising you an escape method?

They thought highly of Spencer and they died. They all died.

"You're dying and I went through all of this with you, but I don't even know your name," I whispered in retrospect.

"Eurydice," she coughed out as a tree branch wrapped around her neck from under my control.

Chapter Fourteen

Search Box

I decided the best way to word the feeling that was sinking down in my chest was guilt. I felt guilty that Eurydice had to die.

I wasn't expecting her to die. I didn't want her to die.

But I didn't have the fortune to think that way. I needed to do this for Maybelle. I felt the pressure of wind push against me. I steadied myself as I felt my feet hit the steps to the Tech building. My feet tingled from the drop. I looked up to see the shiny metal of the Tech building up close. From far away the building appeared to be one big, silver box, but the building had carved in impressions. I ran my hand against the curves of the building. I flinched as I saw the metal plate in front of me quickly push into the other metal wall. The sound of the slamming of metal against metal rang in my ears until a pair of blue eyes abruptly appeared in front of my face. *Lauren.*

Lauren was a tall woman. Her chin met the top of my head. To add to her height, Lauren wore strappy, red stilettos. She appeared coordinated. Her shoes matched her nails which matched the shade on her thin lips. Her hands stayed rested, neatly folded together. Her shoulders were pressed back, making her posture appear professional. The building was much colder than outside from what I could feel from the crisp air blowing on my face and Lauren's face depicted that. There was no color on her face, except for the paint on her lips. Her hair neatly framed the soft edges on her washed-out face. Her hair was a pale blonde that closely resembled Maybelle's hair color. She was very similar to Maybelle despite her ashen appearance. There was an uncanny likeness between the two. The only difference that stood out was Lauren's softer features. Lauren also reminded me of Elaine because of the way she carried herself. But instead of being straitlaced, her aura gave off elegance. Lauren glared at me with her gray eyes and I could already tell she didn't like me.

"There you are, Mia. The Tech in the back has your Search Box." Lauren finger-combed her untangled, blonde hair.

"Is it okay if I look around at the Tech Building?" I asked. I wanted to figure out more about the Techs and was hoping to run into one.

"Don't ruin anything."

No promises.

Lauren shifted slightly to briskly walk past me, and out of the Tech Building.

I looked ahead of me to where Lauren had stood. There was an elegant gold chair that rested against one of the open walls in the rotunda. I looked to the left and there was a marble patterned tiled wall. I placed my hand on it, feeling the cold, smooth texture of the wall. Although the outside in High Tide was dimly lit, the interior was brightened by hanging strings of lights around the window dome. Bits of sand were stuck to the edges of the window. I walked down the hall, my fingers still on the brick pattern, until I saw a white metal door. The door was partially open, so I peered inside. There was no one inside, so I pressed my fingers behind the door to push it open. The room had the same marble wall pattern as the wall on the outside, leading to a marble dome with a hexagon-shaped window on top.

Looking down, I saw a wall that was covered with flat screens. They were all attached by cords to a cherry wood desk that had only one keyboard. It seemed to connect to the biggest computer that laid right above it. The computer screen had a message that threatened to make the computer fall asleep. I walked up to the computer and shook the marble mouse with orange lining to wake up the computer. On the computer was a set-up JavaScript labeled *Rose, Category: Sea Creature 101*. I looked to the right and found a note that said, "Not able to attack without direct command from a Neutral." I stood in front of the computer in awe of the code, and after a few minutes the computer fell asleep

When I turned around, I crashed into a dirty, blonde-haired kid. I lost balance and slightly tripped over the top of my shoes. I took a sigh of relief as I held myself up by leaning my left hand against the cool wall. I could feel the wall almost soak up the warmth from my hand. My eyes widened as the kid dropped the book that he was holding. The book fell with a loud, smacking sound. It vibrated through the room. *How many pages are in that book?* Blue, gridded pages slipped down from inside the book to my boots. I recognized some of the places drawn out on the thin blueprints, such as the rock Marissa once sat on, the Tech building, the pillars surrounding the water, and some of the forests. *He's coding High Tide. He's a Tech.*

I bent over to help the boy pick up his items. I reached for the blueprints as he heaved to lift the book. He continued to situate his arms under the book until he seemed comfortable enough to carry it properly.

"Watch where you're going because that book could seriously hurt someone," I hissed at him. He snorted and furrowed his eyebrows in response, "You're not supposed to be here."

I looked over at him. He matched Lauren with the theme

of white. He wore a white collared shirt and matching basketball shorts that fell to the end of his knees. To match with all of that, his nails were painted white as well. The paint was shiny but it wasn't evenly coated. The ends of his short nails were more opaque. However, he didn't meet Lauren's elegance despite his coordination. His shorts were badly creased in multiple directions and the ends of the porous athletic fabric of his shorts curled up. His shirt seemed to be a naturally stiff article of clothing and had fewer creases excluding the stretched-out collar of the shirt. The collar seemed to end right under his Adam's apple. The buttons on the shirt pointed in different directions. Upon the top of his shirt was a gold name badge. His name was written on it: *Kace.*

Not wanting to upset Kace again, I made sure to keep a matter-of-fact tone as I spoke. "I was looking for the Tech that has the Search Box. You're Kace, right?"

Kace glared at me, looked down at his badge, and then went right back to staring through me. "No. My name is Lauren," he said dryly. He seemed less annoyed with me and more amused as the corner of his lips slightly lifted up. He walked to the desk so he could set the book down on the table. The table slightly shook at the newfound weight on it.

"Very funny," I deadpanned. "Do you have the Box?"

Kace smiled. His upper lip curled in when he smiled, making his bottom lip look bigger than his top one. His lips were a brighter pink at the center and were paler at the edges. He had a straight nose that led up towards his downturned eyes that signaled his need for sleep. He had long eyelashes that pointed downwards, which added to the droopy look to his eyes. His eyebrows were thin and brown, despite his blonde hair. His hair was on the shorter side, slightly brushing over his forehead. His hair was a toned pale-colored blonde with no hints of red or dark shades.

Despite his lifeless colored hair, his lips and the top of his cheeks were pigmented with a light pink.

He oftentimes gestured with his left hand and seemed to guide himself with the same hand. The nails on his right hand looked neater rather than the paint spilling onto the skin around his nails on his left hand. It was easy to assume he was left-handed.

Kace reached for his left pocket to reach for what I assumed to be the Search Box. "Yes, I have it." Kace continued his smile, yet showed less of his teeth. He pulled his hand away from his pocket to gesture towards me. "You're the one working with Maybelle."

My eyes narrowed. Was that how people were going to address me now? "That's me," I huffed.

I wasn't the type to follow someone's lead. I was arrogant in the way I wanted everything to go my way and this was the first time I put my arrogance down. For Maybelle. Not Maybelle herself, but what she promised me. I was going to get my mother back and I didn't care what I had to do.

Kace noticed my discomfort and spoke again. "I didn't mean it in a bad way. I've been here for two years and I haven't seen anyone take Maybelle's side. It's smart and it keeps you safe. I like how you think."

It wasn't my choice.

I was curious about Kace now. He seemed lazy and ignorant despite his laborious work as a Tech. It confused me. "You've been here for two years? How did you get here?" I asked him, shifting my head faintly.

Kace's smile slightly faltered as he scoffed, "You're in for a long story."

"I've got time," I stated.

"Fine." He exposed his palms at me in a very lame attempt at jazz hands. "How Kace Striker got into this dump."

Chapter Fifteen

How Kace Got Into This Dump

The teacher's voice was very annoying. Kace groaned. Ten seconds into the class and the teacher was already halfway through explaining the project. Why even bother going into the classroom? It was almost as if the teacher started class early just to make a mockery out of him. Kace leaned back to allow his back to rest against the wooden doorway. Kace moved his head slightly towards the teacher who was already glaring at him. He huffed as he placed his balance on his feet again. The boy walked over to the desk on his right side. He placed his fingers on the burgundy, plastic chair to pull it towards him before pausing, sighing, and then sitting down. This time, two of his nails were painted on by a blue permanent marker. On his right hand of course. Kace grit his teeth together.

The teacher smiled at the class before speaking. "I need to do a few things, so discuss the topic you want to do amongst yourselves." The teacher walked towards Kace, kneeling next to his desk. "I noticed you came in late again today. Is there a reason for this?" the teacher whispered.

Oh great. The talk about reaching your full potential. He got that talk from a teacher every so often.

Kace sighed, "I guess I walked slowly." He pressed his bottom lip up and shrugged.

"Kace, I notice you get A's in my class, but I would like you to actually participate! If you get As now, imagine after working hard! You'll be able to reach your full potential. If you want to talk about it, feel free to reach me after class or by email."

Called it.

The teacher's sentences sounded more like a speech than sincerity. His words were planned and not genuine. This annoyed Kace.

"Got it. Thanks." Kace pressed his lips together to show his discontent towards his teacher.

"You're working with Charlotte. She'll explain the project." The teacher grinned while showing Kace two thumbs up.

Kace looked at the far end of the classroom to see Charlotte conversing with a classmate beside her. Charlotte had shiny black hair that fell to the center of her back. It was straight with some bevel to it. Charlotte's sweatpants matched the color of her hair. She wore a red paperboy hat that was placed backward on her head. It sort of matched the burgundy sweater that matched the chair more than it did her hat. The sweater had a red and black argyle print with snowflakes on it. He glanced at her sideways. It was April. The weather wasn't even slightly cold. Charlotte smiled at her sister, Megan, at the front center of the room. She glowered back at her before continuing to ignore her. They made it clear that they were sisters and not twins, but their looks were very similar. Megan had the same hair, the same brown eye color, the same amount of melanin, and even the same downturned nose. The only difference was Megan's slanted eyes compared to Charlotte's small and beady ones. Charlotte also had a roundness to her cheeks while Megan had more clear cheekbones. Megan was resting her face on her palms. She wore a gray sweatshirt and gray shorts and looked more put together than Charlotte did even though it seemed as though Charlotte put in more effort. Charlotte walked over to me as the teacher made his way to the front of the classroom. Megan stood behind her sister.

Kace looked at Megan, "Don't you have a partner?"

"They're sick," Megan said matter-of-factly. She put her hands in her sweatshirt pocket, pulling down her sweatshirt a bit.

Charlotte's deskmate sat down next to her partner, feet away from them. Charlotte sat at the desk next to Kace and pulled it towards her friend as she waved. They continued to discuss their prior conversation. Charlotte's movements were big and her facial expressions were lively. She was definitely engaged in the conversation which proved her extroverted nature. Her friend continued to listen by smiling, laughing, and nodding.

Does she ever shut up?

Kace leaned in to listen to her conversation.

"Did you hear about the two people that disappeared?" Charlotte's friend gossiped. For once, Charlotte fell silent. "I heard they're kidnapping young adults to start a new society or something."

Megan sneered, "You could call it that."

The girl gasped. "Why? Do you know about it?"

Megan looked at Kace and then furrowed her eyebrows. "No. I, uh, thought you were talking about something else."

"Hmm. Anyway, I heard it's like Noah's Ark. One of each sex has been missing from each state."

By now, Kace had gotten good at tuning them out. He sat on the floor waiting for the bell to ring.

But something about what the girl said about the disappearances gnawed at him.

And it still gnawed at him while he was walking home.

"Kace."

Kace whipped his head around to see Megan behind him, her face drained of color from the cold. Her hair blew in front of her face, getting stuck on her lips. She tried to brush the hair out of her face with no luck as the strands of hair kept blowing back to their original position. Charlotte was behind her, hastily trying to get her jacket on.

Megan didn't look up at Kace when she spoke to him, her eyes fixated on his boots that sunk slightly in the airy snow below them. "Can we talk?"

Chapter Sixteen

Transparent Bridges Aren't Safe

Kace pressed his lips together and cocked his head in front of him then towards Charlotte. "This is a river."

"Yep! Watch!" Charlotte turned towards the river. The river was fast-paced, yet boulders blocked most of the path, causing water to spew up. Although he was feet away from the river, Kace was able to feel the cool specks of water that traveled from the river. As he walked towards the water the ground seemed to sink in slightly every time he tried to take a step. "Code B," Charlotte said clearly with redundant enthusiasm.

A clear goopy substance seemed to be sucked out of the sloshy grass. The liquid traveled and spread across to the other side, remaining the same transparency. However, it did seem more solid.

Charlotte pointed to the other side. "Sorry for the walk, but once you cross we can teleport."

Kace raised his eyebrows. "We can what?"

Megan interrupted, "She's getting ahead of herself. Just cross the bridge."

Kace used his flexed left hand to point at the bridge. If you could call it that. "That bridge is transparent."

Megan sighed, "I'm tired of you. Cross the damn bridge."

A sickly-sweet voice from a distance was audible. "I already did!" Kace pushed out the air from his lungs as he turned towards Charlotte, who was waving at the both of them. She gave a thumbs-up to Kace. "You got this!"

Megan snorted as Kace looked back at her. "Come on, Kace. I'll cross with you."

Kace stepped forward towards the bridge. A lining of mud seeping from the grass coated the edges of his shoes. The air was damp and smelled of dirt and soil. The splashing water from the river dampened his clothes. His navy sweater now had marks of water droplets, but they didn't sink through. The water spraying on his face made him feel lucky that he opted for his contacts and not his glasses today. He rubbed at his cheek with his left hand covered by his sweater. It was a decently warm day but the mist from the river made him shiver as he stepped even closer to the bridge. Looking closer at the bridge it didn't look real. The goopy substance was gridded like it was computer-generated. The bridge was glossy and strips of reflected light shone off. Although Kace was promised that he wouldn't fall through if he walked on it, it looked like he would slide off the bridge just by trying to balance on it. With his sleeve, Kace pulled up his damp hair that stuck to his face. The boy took his foot and pressed it down on the bridge. But the bridge didn't give the satisfying feeling of pressing your foot on hard ground. The bridge didn't feel like it was holding Kace up, however his foot stayed in place. It was harder to keep balance on the bridge, almost like Kace needed to hold himself up when stepping on it. Kace placed his left foot on the bridge to meet his right. He bent his knees so that he wouldn't topple over. His right foot trembled as he took another step. You're fine, nothing happened. Kace sucked a breath in before continuing to walk normally. Despite the muddy grass at the other side of the bridge, Kace hesitantly placed his foot on the grass in front of him. But looking carefully at the grass, it wasn't green. Blades of dry blue, purple, and red grass stabbed at Kace's ankle. The grass had only those flat blades and they grew in patches. Some areas had longer pieces, some shorter, and some areas only had dirt. The red and purple seemed to grow together and the blue seemed to grow in different areas. Kace rubbed the top of his shoe against the red and purple patch of grass in front of him.

Kace looked up at Charlotte and pointed below him. "What is this grass? Why is it...so...?"

Charlotte looked over Kace's shoulder to see Megan walk up behind Kace, ignoring Kace who was pressing the top of his shoe to the bed of grass below him. Kace quickly turned his head behind him to see Megan tying up her damp hair from the water that splashed everywhere from the flowing river. Kace slowly turned his head up. Kace flinched at the sky, bringing his arms towards his chest. "Why is it so dark? Why is the sky like that? It's..." Kace paused to abruptly slap his sweater out of his way to see his black-colored digital watch on his wrist. The screen wouldn't turn on.

Megan placed her hand on Kace's shoulder. "Time doesn't work here."

Kace was hyperventilating now. "What do you mean time doesn't work here? Where are we?"

"We aren't on Earth," Megan calmly stated. Kace furrowed his eyebrows and gestured his arms towards the bridge. He opened his mouth to speak, but decided against it.

Charlotte started grinning again as Kace whined. Charlotte's voice was sweet and high-pitched as she talked. "We are underground on earth, so we are on the same planet. But we are not in the world, Earth." Kace pressed his eyebrows together. Charlotte continued to talk before Kace could speak. "Earth is strictly above ground. High Tide is in the lithosphere. Physically, we are all on the same planet. Does that make sense?"

Kace squeezed his eyes shut before opening them again and looking back at Charlotte. "I'm sorry. What?"

Charlotte sighed, yet maintained her cheerful appearance, only with a more tired look to her droopy eyelids. "This world was accidentally computer-engineered by Techs." Charlotte pointed behind Kace. "And thus we need something computer-engineered to enter. Everything here is computer-generated. It's called High Tide for its computerized source of water. It was originally created to solve overpopulation, but there are not enough resources on High Tie for more than one percent of people on Earth. Techs continue to design High Tide to keep it working. That's where you come in."

"So you brought me here to work a full-time job? I don't even make it to class on time." Kace looked at Charlotte skeptically.

Megan weakly exhaled as a form of a scoff. "Pretty much. I don't like it either." Megan opened her mouth to suck a breath in, but kept her teeth pressed together. She pressed her lips together. "They overwork us, so you get that," Megan said sarcastically, "but that's not all. There's a challenge each year to give heirs of the Royalty here the chance to overtake the Royalties' positions. Maybelle, one of the Queens, has total control of High Tide currently. Obstacles provide challenges before you are ready to go up against the Queens. Oftentimes the obstacles block exits as well. Maybelle blocks out the exits, so those who want to escape and not partake are forced to deal with her. And Maybelle has never lost a battle."

Charlotte chimed in enthusiastically, "But she can't block out the Trap!"

Megan glared at her. "There's an obstacle there too. They're living human obstacles but they've been modified.

Anyone who commits a High Tide crime is sent there. So you either die there, die from a computer-generated monster, or die in Maybelle's hands. No one has escaped. They're beating kids to their death. It's wrong. Maybelle blocks the exits so no one is able to know of her exploitation. But who would believe a snotty teenager with claims of a new world anyway?" Megan pressed her lips together.

"So you're saying the moment I start this job, I won't be able to leave it," Kace clarified.

Megan grumbled, "We don't get paid either."

Charlotte smiled to try and ignore the prior discussion. "Anyway, all you need to know is how to code! I'll bring you to the building. Code AA2." She seemed passionate about her rant about High Tide. There was a shining look to her eyes and it inspired Kace.

Kace's heart sunk as he felt the feeling of free-falling when he fell on his knees against the prickly grass. His knees left a stinging feeling along with a zig-zag print etched into his skin from the grass. Kace looked up and came face to face with a big piece of metal.

Charlotte, who had landed on her feet being her graceful self, bounced over to a tablet. The middle portion of the tablet was covered in a stack of gray tape to sloppily tape it to the building. Charlotte placed the tips of her fingers on the top of the tablet that wasn't covered in duct tape. The tablet glowed green to show that it recognized her. The metal plate side of the building slammed into the right side, leaving an opening for them to walk through.

Why was Kace involved with this? He didn't want anything to do with the job he was appointed to and he definitely did not want to be affiliated with any sort of a revolution for that would mean he would have to work. He didn't want to do anything, even on Earth, so why would he be suited for the job? Didn't they see the type of personality he had?

Chapter Seventeen

Why Kace Was Carrying the Biggest Book in the World

Kace didn't even want to untangle the knot of the two strings tied around the book in front of him. There was no doubt that he didn't want to go over the pages of the book nor imagine picking the book up. Kace wondered how many pages were in the book, but to check the last page he'd have to untie the knot and then push the earlier pages away to see the number on the corner of the last page.

Megan had just set down the book in front of him with no explanation. She had also turned on an abnormally large desktop that hung on the wall in front of him. The screen was dark, set at a low brightness, and showed a dark screen. The dark screen had a JavaScript typed in red that Kace did not understand. Kace looked around him, the number of computers in the room was overwhelming. The different sized desktops were all connected by multiple tied-up wires that traveled throughout the walls of the room and were taped up for hazardous reasons. It was unusual to imagine that everything he saw here was coded in the powered-on computer in front of him. Nothing here was completely real, just automatically brought to life by a line of connected computers. The bridge they walked on earlier? It wasn't real. The plastic white chair he was sitting in? Also fake. Everything here was. Except for maybe the people here. But their magical abilities didn't exist either. Everyone here was modified to some extent. Meaning they had to be coded into the computer to even enter High Tide. And when you enter anyone on the computer, you can modify them to fit your needs. Meaning you could add magical powers to their abilities.

Kace's code script was open on the laptop lying next to his computer. The screen was darkening to warn Kace that the screen would go completely dark soon. Unable to understand the script, Kace didn't understand what it said about him, but Charlotte said he could teleport and he couldn't really do anything, but take her word for it. The oxygen he was breathing in this world didn't even exist either; they were underground. So, it was safe for Kace to assume that oxygen was coded into one of the computers as well. Also, the fact that one wrong moment related to the computers near him could threaten his income of oxygen was completely terrifying. Kace groaned and slammed his forehead against the book. He didn't want to question his existence because of a computer either. He didn't want to do anything. The force of his fall caused the desk to rattle. The cords on the desk made the computers slightly shake which alarmed Kace, but he didn't move. The whirring sound that noted that the computers were still operating properly suddenly stopped. Kace pushed air out from his lips to calm his heart rate down. His lungs continued to heave out of adrenaline, but he was still able to calm down slightly after a few deep breaths. He let out a sigh once the computers generated the calming white noise again.

Kace pressed his forehead with more force towards the

book. The itchiness of the knotted twine rubbed lines on his forehead, causing him discomfort. He lifted his head barely to rest it against his arm instead. Kace groaned, understanding that he had to do work. He used his arm to push his head up. He rubbed at the new couple of dents on his forehead. He brought his hand down to the knot on the book. He slid his nail in the opening of the loop of twine. The coarseness of the twine burned his fingers as he tried to pull it apart. Gently pushing the twine away, he pressed the tips of his fingers to the edge of the book, curling his fingers over the flap. The book had a fabric protectant over the entire cover and was very textured. It felt like burlap. The fabric had small little openings, exposing the dark mahogany color of the book. Kace huffed as he used his left hand to push off the book slightly from the desk. He reached for the bottom of the book to remove the fabric cover. The cover was a deep red-brown leather material. Etched in gold was the word Codes. Maybe it would explain the foreign script in front of him. The corners of the book were slightly blunt and frayed.

He pulled a string of the cover's material from the fraying bottom edge of the book. Setting the burlap fabric cover aside, he pushed the cover to the left. Blank. The page was blank. Kace didn't believe that Megan would hand him a blank book with that many pages. It didn't have the lines of a journal either. The pages were textured but they were too thin to be drawing pages. The book was too big for it to be anything common. The side of the book made it seem like it had words and pictures because of the thin streaks of black and different colors. He flipped over some more of the off-white pages with some determination now. Nothing. One page had a coffee stain that wrinkled the page and a couple of pages underneath it, but the weight of the book had mostly flattened it out. The slightest smell of coffee lingered on the book. Yet there were no words.

Kace stood up to slam the rest of the pages to his left to see the past page, pushing the chair behind him with his calves. Again, nothing. Kace gripped his hand around the armrest of the white chair to bring it forward. He fell back to the chair, heaving to lift up the book that he slid off from the table in the process. His muscles hurt trying to work against gravity. The thought of the book falling on his legs had pained his legs even though they weren't harmed. Kace unintentionally slammed the book down on the table on the other side of the laptop after heaving to pick up the book. It seemed impossible to set the book down gently and the weight of the book seemed to weigh on his chest making it hard to breathe. Kace pressed down on his knuckles, hearing the satisfying crack from them. The feeling relaxed him. Kace wrapped his hands around the adjustable neck of the gray lamp in front of him. He pushed it towards him and aimed the light down. Using his middle finger and thumb he twisted power button and a white light shined down on the desk. Kace shoved the book into position under the light and pushed the cover down again. The circle of light the lamp created allowed words to appear in the designated area. The words in the book matched the color of the cover. They seemed hand-written in the book. Everything was listed in bullet points. The first page was titled, "Ability Assistance." The bullet right underneath it was the code Kace recognized Charlotte was using. Code AA2-teleportation (visualize the place you would like to visit). Kace ran his hand along the side of the book. His hand stopped at the feel of a page that didn't have the same gritty texture as the rest of the book. He pinched the paper towards him, lifting a couple of pages that were on top of it so that the paper wouldn't rip. He placed the paper underneath the light.

Neutrals—Have the ability of all the current Queens and Techs (e.g., water manipulation, fire invulnerability and manipulation, nature manipulation, and teleportation). They are typically heirs of Marissa.

Heirs of Maybelle—Typically have a nature manipulation ability.

Heirs of Nerissa—Typically have a water manipulation ability.

Heirs of Allison—Typically have a fire invulnerability and manipulation ability.

Techs—Code for High Tide. Are not descendants to the Queens and are chosen randomly, thus are not able to compete or escape.

*No High Tide competitors are direct descendants of the Royalty. The Royalty do not reproduce. Instead, they are relatives of their family.

Goals for Kace Striker 10-12-15:

1) Design an obstacle that only Neutrals can control.
2) Code the newly created obstacle.*

*Directions to code are in the last few pages of the book.

Kace took pride in his creativity. He now understood what it meant to be a Tech.

Kace smiled his bottom-lipless smile as he bit the shiny cap off his drawing pen.

Chapter Eighteen

Since When?

Kace didn't draw much. The laziness didn't help with that either. But colored pencil in hand, paper on table, his ideas seemed to come to life without the effort of art. His orange pencil seemed to dance elegantly through the indigo color he had just used. The pencil seemed to flow on the page without the force of friction. Kace could almost sense the presence of the animal. The soft textured pale yellow underneath that felt like a snake. The scattered specks of orange on its stomach. The puffiness of the gills and how they gracefully opened to exhale. The wide mouth of the creature that reached to the sides of its face. The ovalish purple tongue that was exposed whenever the animal inhaled. The shimmering indigo scales that gracefully moved alongside its gills. The smooth scarlet red of the round plates on its back. The flexible fins looked so detailed it was almost like Kace could touch the drawing. It was almost like Kace could see the animal twist around in the air; its fins moving to the rhythm of the flow of air around him.

To code the animal didn't take that much time. In under twenty minutes, Kace was able to press the arrow on the corner of the screen to save it into the database. A white pop-up asked for background information. Kace pulled the keyboard closer to him, resting his fingers on the home row.

Name: Rose.
Relation to Royalty: Marissa's pet.
Notes: Can only be controlled by a Neutral.

Kace used the mouse next to him to guide the cursor to the done button. But what happens when the computer accepts the code? Where does the animal appear?

The situational irony would have been funny if Kace wasn't scared to death by the pair of yellow eyes in front of him. The animal was currently calm, its mouth partially open showing its purple tongue. Each scale on the creature was reflective. Kace's sharp features looked softer under the blue appearance of the animal's scales. His once sharp nose appeared rounded under the trance of the scales. Kace reached up to touch the tip of his nose gently with his forefinger. Kace looked up, remembering that the creature was in fact alive. The adrenaline flowing through his body allowed him to feel each thump his heart created. He tensed up, bracing himself for some sort of impact.

It relieved Kace when he realized that he never coded offensive or defensive behaviors into Rose. He relaxed, shaking his head at himself. It almost seemed like Rose was more afraid of him. The animal stayed a two-foot distance away from Kace. Kace slowly shifted the back of his hand towards Rose's face. Rose's nose twitched slightly as it sniffed Kace. Now more comfortable with Kace, the animal brought its face closer to his. Kace brought his hand to the scales on his neck.

Kace's eyebrows furrowed as he saw an unusual movement on Rose's scales. As if they were trying to show him something. Kace turned so he could see the scales better. The once reflective scales were now producing a visualization. A very young girl was sitting on a boulder. The scene didn't look realistic, as if it was edited with a tint of blue. Like wearing a pair of blue sunglasses. The rock was unusually curved inwards and was on the flatter side except for the mounds of rock on the sides. The rock was very porous, which created texture and was a dull brown-gray. The girl was sitting on the indent of the sea boulder. Her knees barely made it to the edge of the boulder from where she was sitting, and her short calves barely hung down. Her toes didn't touch the calm green water below her. The girl made a sort of a pouty face. Her arms were crossed high up near her neck. The scene on the scales changed, depicting the newly created Rose emerging from the water. Her head disrupted the still balance of the water, splashing the little girl slightly. The movement of the water crashed against the boulder, creating sea foam that rested beside the rock. With her stumpy fingers, Marissa wrapped her fingers around Rose's neck lovingly. Marissa gave a goofy and crooked childish smile. The two scenes repeated themselves on the scales of the animal. Rose had now twisted itself in the air to lie down on its back. It rubbed its head against Kace's hand to force the boy to pet it. Kace smiled at the animal, a dimple on his cheek forming showing that he was genuinely smiling.

But it didn't make any sense. The rock still existed but Marissa was now trapped above it, encased in protective smoke. Many people even perceived her to be dead. So how could Rose's envisioning be true? Kace turned to the laptop next to him. He powered off the app that showed his coding analytics. After X-ing out of the page, the live security footage of High Tide appeared. And there was his proof. There was no trace of Marissa, just the assumption she was in the encasing of hovering smoke above the limestone-looking boulder. There were now more boulders similar in style, size, and texture besides the flatter, chair-like boulder Marissa sat on. A wooden flat, dock-like bridge with high railings that were the same deep brown as the planks of the dock.

But what was truly mystical was the smoke that has been claimed to have held Marissa. The smoke was wispy and flowed around the designated area, but the smoke remained the same oval-like shape. Parts of the remaining oval shape of the smoke seemed to twist and turn; none of it stayed at the same area constantly. The fog at times seemed gray, but curiously at times also looked red.

He was told that Maybelle and Marissa had a fight, which resulted in Marissa being trapped. But what could a five-year-old child have done? How did Maybelle have the power to conceal Marissa?

He concluded that the Queens had to have extra abilities that they chose to hide. The computers provided the ability to modify anything in someone. Lauren was able to change people's abilities within a few minutes.

With Lauren being a Queen with full control over the Techs, full loyalty from Lauren is needed to do anything. Maybelle had the advantage of Lauren on her side. Maybelle was powerful, but anytime she felt threatened she'd attack. That was wrong.

A slight change in water flow startled Kace. That had never happened before. A bright crimson color caught his eye. Rose. Kace quickly twisted behind him, keeping his hands gripped onto the desk. Rose wasn't in the room anymore. He had just altered the past of High Tide. The event Kace had just seen was the past he had just modified.

His sense of power withholding the computer was alarming.

Kace peeled his sweaty fingers off the desk and turned back towards the computer. His cursor rested on a file with a name that was too long to see without clicking on the file. All he could see was: Do Not Open. *Well now it was just asking him to open the file, wasn't it?*

Chapter Nineteen

Why Does It Matter?

High Tide is also known as the Land of the Healing. It was named High Tide after the newest queen's special power. When she was lifted from her rock, she was preserved in a bubble and the former Queen of the Sea was lifted from her curse. Now as a human, she is still not a Queen. Queen Maybelle and Queen Allison are the only Queens left. However, no one knows where Queen Allison is. The two Queens on the day of the healing decided to cast a spell so that they would never age. Nerissa had to promise something to Queen Maybelle in exchange for letting her be in the state. We talked to Maybelle in an interview.

The next line in the text said, Read more.

Kace turned back, his new automatic reflex, to make sure no one was behind him. It was obvious that the article was old, still referring to Marissa as a current Queen. However, the article seemed to withhold valuable information and had to be guarded for a good reason. Kace pressed his bottom lip out, debating on if the read was worth the risk. He did a quick scan behind him before reaching towards the black sleek mouse in front of him, realizing there was no one behind him. He looked back again. Nothing. His quick-paced heartbeat made his chest heave with worry.

Maybelle said that four people were blessed with powers

by being High Tide Kids. Although she won't tell us who blessed the children. We also talked to Jayde, one of the main police officers in High Tide. She said that High Tide is in danger in ways she can't talk about and that the prophecy-

"Kace!" someone called. Kace scrambled to quickly close out of the page, as his hand shivered from the sickly cold feeling that spread through his body. He rubbed the cold sweat off his hands on his neck as he reached for the power-down button on the side of the computer. Rubbing his hand on his neck did him no good as his neck had droplets of sweat. He felt filthy.

Now face to face with his darker reflection of himself on the empty black screen of the turned-off computer, his self-image wasn't much better. He looked terrible to match his unclean feeling. There was a paleness to his once pigmented lips while his nose still flushed a shade of red. His lower eyelids seemed to droop down from stress and there were dark rings under the bags of his eyes. Kace lightly pressed down on his cold cheeks. His warmer fingertips felt unfamiliar on his frigid face.

Kace recalled the mention of the prophecy in the article. The article must have been written at the time of the first High Tide Challenge. The article mentioned that only four High Tide Kids competed, yet now the challenge had expanded to two people per country. Fewer if there were no eligible descendants of the Queens residing there. Kace was also told that Marissa wrote the first prophecy, but after the event with the child and Maybelle, Lauren took the responsibility for the rest of the challenges.

If there was one thing clear, it was that he completely agreed with Megan. High Tide was a hellhole. There was an eeriness to the situation in High Tide. Something he couldn't put his finger on. Maybelle. Maybelle kept the information in the article from falling into the hands of most people for a reason. And how could an adult feel so threatened by a five-year-old child? Kace's top lip curled over as he turned his head towards the laptop to see the remains of Marissa. Maybelle was definitely the scary type, but murdering someone was unbelievable. Murdering a child. He didn't like this one bit. He didn't like High Tide. He didn't like Lauren. And he most definitely did not like Maybelle.

Kace drew a fast breath in. He tried to keep his voice calm and called back, "Yeah?"

The only thing he could do was be compliant.

Chapter Twenty

You're Welcome

"The end. Now I really should get going." His arm fell down at his side before noticing the bump in his pocket. He reached into his pocket, realizing what I was going to say before I interrupted him. He pulled out a rectangular silver metal object. He threw it up and caught it as he spoke, "This is the Search Box you were looking for." He twirled in his hands. "It's kind of like a calculator."

I guess the object resembled a calculator without a screen or buttons. So, it looked like a slab of metal and not like a calculator at all. But, from a distance the two objects could easily be comparable, being the same size and shape. At what I assumed to be the top of the object, there was a tiny plastic dome that covered a small blinking purple LED light. Kace pointed it towards me as I reached for it. His grip wasn't tight and it was easy to pull the object away from him.

I blinked at him, holding the Search Box that Maybelle needed in my hand. I watched as Kace set his right foot down, his back facing me, his heel causing a slight sound against the smooth floor.

A thin layer of saliva coated my teeth and tongue since I had stayed silent during Kace's story. I pressed my tongue against my two front teeth, my tongue hitching over the gap between them. I swiped the spit-coating off my teeth with my tongue to get ready to speak, "Hey." I grabbed his arm. "Don't leave without allowing me to say anything. I have questions."

Kace raised his eyebrows. "I gave you the Box. I'll pass on the questions." Kace smiled and pushed out a breath in a form of a half-hearted laugh. His smile made his top lip curl inwards, smile lines forming on the edges of his upper lip. For a boy who obviously steered away from communicating, he sure smiled a lot.

"You're the only one here who can give me answers to my questions. I can't just sit here in this world without knowing anything about it." I closed my partially open mouth to pause before speaking again. "I have a deal for you. I know a way to help you get out. I can cover for you from Lauren. Just first answer my questions, okay?"

Kace's breath hitched. I knew my sentence would surprise him. Why would I be worried about him when I could help myself escape? He furrowed his eyebrows together, yet nodded his head softly to agree with my proposition. He took a step forward; he was now intrigued.

I didn't wait for him to speak before I started again. "You said each person competing has to be a descendant to one of the Royalty. So am I related to Marissa, and Spencer is related to Allison?"

Kace chuckled. "I said they have to be a descendant, but I never said I have to code the same power in the High Tide Kids as their relatives. *You* might be related to Marissa, however, it would be strange to give the guy who has a discomfort towards rain storms a water manipulation ability, wouldn't it?"

Kace snorted at my newly contorted face; he knew his statement would shock me. It was so obvious, yet I never noticed Spencer's similarity to Nerissa. Their features were too comparable for comfort. The same hair (although

Nerissa had dyed portions of her hair red, they both had the same close to black hair), the same aquiline nose, and the same pushed in heart-shaped lips. The only noticeable difference was Spencer's green eyes compared to Nerissa's dark ones. Nerissa's eyes attracted light; her eyes glittered in the sun. While Spencer's eyes seemed to push brightness away, making his eyes look bolder. The skin around Nerissa's eyes lifted and accented them while Spencer's eyes were more wide-set.

It wasn't only their appearance that was so similar. They both had unique personalities. Nerissa was quick with words with vocabulary and by having a sharp tongue. And although Spencer liked to steer away from assertive sentences, it was easy for him to speak spontaneously with a quick-witted attitude. It made more sense for his personality to match Nerissa's rather than Allison's bolder responses. Allison had no concern whether or not people liked her and that definitely did not reflect on Spencer.

Everyone liked Spencer, even the people who died at the Trap for him. Allison, on the other hand, wasn't afraid to be disliked.

"What happens when you die here?"

"Well, *death* is subjective," Kace stated, half-heartedly.

"What do you mean by that?"

"First of all, it's harder to die here. On Earth, we hear about death due to injuries, but unless death happens on impact, that's not likely to happen here."

"Why are you avoiding this question, Kace?"

He scoffed at the use of his name.

"I don't know, okay? I don't know what happens when you die. It's not like a dream where when you die you wake up back on Earth. But, as I said, death is subjective. Injury is impossible to occur here, but I'm not sure death is the same." He paused, looking for a reaction from me before he continued. "I'm not smart enough to check how death was coded into High Tide on the computers." He looked at the computers as if they were going to give him some sort of answer.

"So, they're dead. They're completely dead."

"All the competitors die. It happens in every competition. We don't know what happens to them after. There are no corpses. That's the only evidence that we have that they don't actually pass away as they do on Earth."

I looked at him. "You're a Tech. You're supposed to have more evidence. You have the computers right there."

He laughed in a very unfriendly way, "Well, it's not like I chose to be here, Mia. I'd rather not spend my time contemplating what happens when I die here."

He looked me up and down as if I was accusing him of something he hadn't done, his eyes staying locked when he looked at mine.

Kace continued again, "Don't you have Maybelle to give you this information?"

I didn't want to answer that question.

"Do even you want to escape, Kace? You don't seem to hate this place as much as you say you do." I cocked my head to the side.

Kace grinned at me, cocking his head to the side to mock me, "You didn't answer my question."

Childish. Why was he laughing at a situation like this?

I sucked a breath in. "Maybelle tells me what she wants to—" I exhaled before continuing. "—You complain about being here, but I think you like it here."

"I think your introspection is wrong. I hate it here and I'm only answering these questions to get out."

He leaned against the wall, waiting for me to continue talking.

"I'm never leaving here."

He raised his eyebrows, pretending to be shocked by my answer. "You won't be able to leave after the bomb lights. I'm sure you'll re-think your choice before then."

"I seriously doubt that."

He shook his head as he laughed. "Right, Maybelle's helping you with your mom. She'll need my help to initiate that."

"She'll need Lauren's help." I narrowed my eyes.

Kace shrugged. "The challenge only ends when the grenade lights. You'll need to figure out how to light the grenade to finish the challenge so that any of this can start." I sniffed before he continued. "The past competitors light it in the back room." Kace gestured his head to the back door, tucked away behind the computers. "Most of them don't make it, so we'll see how it goes for you."

I huffed, "You're saying that if I want to end this challenge, I have to light a grenade which would kill me anyway."

"Hmm, no." Kace seemed to contemplate if it was possible if I'd die or not. "I think you'd make it. They don't die due to an explosion; the grenade creates a final obstacle like the other creatures you've been fighting here."

"What happens to the ones who make it?"

"They get killed off," Kace snorted. "The Queens are very fond of their positions. If there's a threat to their downfall, you can expect hostility."

"I don't need to expect hostility. I don't want to be a Queen."

"Then you'll be perfect."

"What do you mean by that?"

Kace leaned towards me to cup my shoulder. He pointed to the security camera feed playing on the computers as he spoke, "They get mad when the grenade gets anywhere near the water. I wonder what happens when you light it there. If you're not worried about taking their positions after the grenade lights, this job is perfect for you. "

"If anything upsets Maybelle, she wouldn't uphold her part of the deal of bringing my mom back. I can't do that."

Kace scoffed. "Come on, it's just a bit of fun. What's a bomb underwater going to do? Kill a couple of fish?"

I crossed my arms. I wanted this conversation done with, my energy completely drained out from Kace's personality. The room reeked of aging paint despite its clean look. I wanted nothing more than to smell the salty outdoors of High Tide again. I needed to get outside. My head hurt and my stomach heaved. *Don't throw up again.*

I clutched my stomach. "You haven't personally met Maybelle, have you?"

"Only vicariously." Kace stepped closer to me before speaking. "But noting that you're talking to me and not her, she doesn't seem like that much help. You'd think you'd look to her for answers and not me. I don't even want to help you."

"You've made that clear," I huffed.

"What has Maybelle given you information on?"

I stepped back, giving space between Kace and me.

"She told me about your creatures and to stay away from the High Tide Police," I clarified.

"That's it?" Kace furrowed his eyebrows. "The High Tide Police aren't dangerous. They're good for enforcing safety and transporting people away from certain locations. Not that you'd need that, since Neutrals can teleport too." Kace rubbed the top of his head and stretched his shoulder by pushing it towards his back. "And I'm sure you've personally met one of my creations already."

"I wish I hadn't," I said, wishing to wipe the egotistical facial expression that he had when he talked about his own work, yet he just continued to grin. I clenched my fist before addressing his other statement. "I guess Maybelle doesn't want the Police to know about how she controls everything here."

"What business?" Kace sneered. "All she does is lock all the exits and reward herself every year because no one was able to escape. That's how the game works."

I dropped my shoulders and gasped at Kace. "Are you saying you agree with her? You think what she's doing is right?"

"What?" Kace looked insulted. "No. I'm just saying she has a right to do so. If anything, she's risking her own position as Queen since escaping is harder than becoming royalty. Do you really think that a survivor from the Challenge wouldn't tell someone about what happened to them? If a competitor was able to escape, they'd be running to the police and the secrecy of High Tide would be exposed."

He snickered, "If High Tide was revealed, trust me, High Tide would be under worse hands than Maybelle's."

"It doesn't matter, the police wouldn't believe them. Maybelle is killing competitors off for no reason."

"People believe anything," Kace huffed. He furrowed his eyebrows, as his face dropped. "And you act as if you're much better, supporting her for your own gain."

"How can you insult me when you are okay with sitting and watching her actions? We're both the same."

"There's a difference. You need to be humbled. I just know my own morals." Kace held his forefinger up, knowing that I was going to argue with him. "Tell me how you want me to get out."

Chapter Twenty-One

Curiosity Killed the Cat

*C*ode DA Woods. *Code Dangerous Areas Woods.* I repeated over and over, the words starting to feel comfortable in my mouth. I remembered that part in Kace's story. I sat below two brooding palm trees, letting the shade wash over me as I fiddled with the bark on one of the trees. I stared at the tall trees that towered over me. Flat, dark green leaves fell down. The leaves were as long as half of my arm, but almost as wide as my torso. I went around the trees. I found a building with a gold-yellow dome. The dome was fading in color as if it had been there for centuries. Thick strips of paint were peeling off in large chunks. There was no door covering the doorway, so I waltzed right in. Each wall was painted with gold, silver, and rose color. The entire set of walls was part of an abstract mural, but on one wall was a bulky gold frame covering some of the art. Writing was etched in it, carefully under the glass. I brushed the back of my hand against the frame before I placed my hand against the glass, noticing more strips of the trimming paint around the edges of the frame. Air blew around me, making a loud sound. It sounded like a plane was passing by. I looked down at my hand and tattooed on my arm were the same words carved in the frame. I looked back at the frame. The lettering slowly disappeared from under the glass.

My breath hitched at the sight of something blonde. I let out a shaky breath at the realization that it was Lauren behind me and not Maybelle. Not that much of an upgrade. I didn't bother to look at her, trying to rub the dark marks off my arm instead. I pressed my upper lip higher as I turned towards the towering woman, thrusting my arm in confusion towards her.

Lauren's features did not contort upon seeing my hand; she kept her usual stoic expression. She reached for my arm and I pulled it away, pressing my eyebrows close together. Lauren being a foot away from me made me very uncomfortable. I didn't mind too much when Maybelle came close to me since she was always the touchy type, always going for a hug or a rub on my arm, but there was nothing human-like in Lauren and being close to her felt odd. As if she wasn't living.

Lauren just barely pouted her bottom lip in disappointment. "All my hard work and it's on your arm."

I sighed to let out my confusion. "Why does it do that? Why did it happen to my arm?" I thrust my pointer finger towards where the inked prophecy used to be.

Lauren looked up at my eyes. "Travel purposes," Lauren stated. "Anything it touches, it appears on. But that shouldn't have happened to you. You're not supposed to be here. Stop rubbing it, it's like a tattoo, its not going to just wipe off. Leave it. It might do you some good." I shook my head while trying to isolate my stained arm from my body. The marks felt irregular. Lauren huffed, "It's just ink, Mia. It might help you."

I nodded, unsure of why some words could benefit me, as Lauren reached into her jumpsuit pocket. Lauren waved her hand half-heartedly by just moving her fingers. In a few seconds, there wasn't any trace of her. She disappeared. She must have coded teleportation in herself in the Tech building. Her teleportation was smooth, a clean disappearance while mine made me feel like I was free-falling. It oftentimes made me collapse. Teleportation was an uncomfortable feeling and Lauren made it seem easy. I looked at a square of white that took Lauren's place. An envelope. I reached for it, the paper crinkling under the force of my nails. In permanent marker were the words: Don't open now! Being impatient, I growled at the fact I had to wait to open it. When would I know when to open it?

Feeling the tingling feeling from my own teleportation, I felt my feet collide with the wood of the bridge over the sea. The green water with specks of white foam rested calmly below me. The landings on my teleportation attempts have gotten better. I laughed subtly, recalling my first attempt at teleportation when I crashed into the water.

I leaned over at the bride's ledge, a warm breeze crashing against my curly hair. My hair was dense and didn't change position too much. The aloof strands of my frizzy hair floated carelessly in the wind. It made my head slightly uncomfortable as I tried to push the strands down with my left hand while using my right hand to slip Lauren's envelope into my pocket. I didn't mind too much. It was nice to get fresh air. The punch of the smell of salty water and the slight smell of damp wood relaxed me.

I never want to go home again if life post-challenge in High Tide is as calm as this.

Chapter Twenty-two

Final or Finale?

I could feel my nails dig into my palms despite the layer of thin fabric cushioning my grip. The material was slippery and felt like polyester. I could see my nails turning white from the pressure on them. I looked up at Kace, whose shirt I had snatched up in my hand. "I told you to team up with Spencer to help you escape. Not—" I gestured at Kace with my left hand, dropping my raised right hand. I could see my nails turning red from the sudden blood flow to my nails. "Not do whatever you did to Spencer. He doesn't want to be a King; he doesn't need to go against Maybelle."

With the lighting dimmer outside than in the Tech room, Kace definitely looked older than me. He looked more mature than Spencer and me and had a particular way of speaking that proved he was above my age level. Kace exhaled with his nose and spoke, his eyes lowering. "How do you know that?"

How did I know that? Well, I didn't. My judgment of Spencer was clouded by my past experiences with him. And with his confrontation with Allison, he had every right to take her spot. But did he want to?

Spencer was seated in front of me, his palms holding up his cheeks. I looked down at the plastic food container in front of me. Four soft grapes were left in it. I picked one up and rolled it in between my thumb and forefinger. The seat I was sitting on was hard and uncomfortable. It was one of those plastic stools that attached to the lunch table. I changed my posture to make myself more comfortable. I looked up at my empty plastic bag that once held my sandwich. I looked across the brown table. The lunch table had a smooth wood pattern with streaks of black and dark brown. Spencer's lunch was already packed into his bag like the obsessive neat freak he was. His partially shut laptop rested beside his right elbow.

Spencer looked extremely tired and he had told me he hadn't slept all night.

"Do you believe in magic, Spence?" I dropped my left hand, still rolling the grape between my fingers.

"Are you serious?" Spencer raised his eyebrows as I nodded. He sat up properly to continue speaking, moving his hands away from his face and straightening his posture. "I mean it's possible if we count the idea of it being human-created. It would still be a theory, not a fact. However, the idea of it being supernatural, that would be—"

I smiled. "I don't believe in magic, so if you don't believe in it, don't sugarcoat it for me."

"No. I'm being honest—"

I interrupted him again. "Did you get a letter last night?"

Spencer wrinkled his face, seemingly shocked that I knew he received something last night. Spencer couldn't lie for the life of him and I could see clearly on his face that he was debating showing me the letter or not. It shocked me that he received a letter too. Was someone trying to prank the both of us? Spencer reached into his pocket and unraveled the neatly folded lined paper; the same signature from the lady, Nerissa, was visible at the bottom. He smiled. He had a wide smile, his lips broadcasting both his shiny top and bottom teeth. He raised his eyebrows lovingly. "This one? Did you get one too?"

I pulled mine out from my water bottle pouch in my

backpack. I placed it on the table smoothing out the crinkled edges that got hit when I moved my backpack around. I smiled back at him. "Yup."

Spencer examined my letter without touching it, shrugged, and continued to grin at me. "I guess we will have to figure out what it's all about together." He shrugged.

I gave him a soft laugh. "You don't really seem like the 'go with the flow' type."

He laughed back at me. "I'm not always uptight—" He stopped when he saw my disagreement as I raised my eyebrows. He rolled his eyes.

I crushed the grape between my fingers and dropped it in the container. I could smell grape juice. I bent over to put my items away then spoke. "That was an oxymoron," I said before Spencer could inform me that it was one. I sat back up. "See, I'm smart." I beamed at Spencer.

Spencer smiled at me, this time not showing his teeth. "You just don't give yourself enough credit."

The memory made my throat seem like it was closing up. It hurt to swallow. Spencer was right about how our abilities were created. Spencer was right about the Trap. Spencer was right about everything. I sighed. It was time to stop interfering with everything he does. So if he wanted to be a King, I wouldn't stop him.

"Well," I raised my eyebrows, "does he want to be a King?"

Kace scoffed, "I don't think so."

I squeezed my eyes shut, already annoyed with him. "Why are you here?"

Kace gave me a childish grin as he let out a *ha*. "What? This wasn't the beach?" he deadpanned. I glared at him and he smiled, slightly upset that I didn't laugh at his joke, before continuing, serious this time. "Here's my plan. Lauren's suspicious of me, so this is perfect. You distract Maybelle. Spencer makes an attack towards Maybelle and then you distract her again while Spencer leaves the scene. It covers up his presence. They'll assume he escaped. Spencer is invisible right now because I gave him a Code from the big codebook. Everything's perfect."

Kace was known for his creativity and that terrified me. The chance of associating with someone who seeks out the truth before making a judgment, with someone more like me who goes with what feels right, was a risk. Kace definitely was not as calculated as Spencer, which was another fear factor of mine. I was used to Spencer always being right.

"No one has escaped before. They're not going to assume that." I raised my eyebrows at Kace.

Kace continued his serious glance at me. "No, they're not. You're going to tell Maybelle that you helped him escape and you provided the distraction so that she wouldn't attack Spencer while he did so."

"I'm not doing that." I wrapped my fingers over my left hand.

Kace glared at me, leaning towards me. "You are. Because otherwise, he escapes legitimately. He has no other way to save himself from Maybelle." Kace tapped my stiffened arm with the side of his forefinger. He smiled slightly. "You don't want that, do you?"

I felt very secretive of my arm with the presence of Lauren nearby when I had the words imprinted on me. Her cold demeanor that shifted to a friendlier one had frightened me. Lauren was there for a reason I was unsure of and that frightened me. None of the words on my arm seemed to connect with me. With Spencer and I not being the large majority of the competitors, the prophecy was mostly written about the other High Tide Children, so there was not much of a point to care. How could I be sure that a section of the prophecy was about me or Spencer? I glanced at some of the rhythmical sentences. I couldn't concentrate on the words on my arm as my head throbbed. *Door. Floor. Mythical. Vocal. Pride. Hide.* My head hurt and my vision seemed to falter to the beat of my throbbing pain. The area around me was tinted with a bit of red. *Why am I seeing red?* Kace's finger stayed rested on the first section. *But a final breath a boy must take. While the rest must ache. On this land, there's no demise. But, to an unfamiliar and edited female's words will he abide? Was this about Spencer?* There was no specific mention of him, yet the other sentences mentioned events that already occurred and this section seemed current. *Why did this one end with a question?* My eyes watered and I tried to push my mass of hair behind me.

My face burned up as I tried to speak, "Unfamiliar and edited—" I sounded spaced-out, even to myself. I wasn't even looking at Kace now. *Edited, like modified by coding like Kace had said? That was the only logical reason for the use of this word.* And there was no other logical reference. "The Trap," I breathed out.

Kace moved the finger he had on my arm and shifted so he could reassure me by slightly shaking my shoulder. He gave a matching reassuring smile, "You'll be fine. He won't leave if you listen to my plan. This will help him. Then we'll figure out how to get me to escape after."

I swallowed and nodded. His unnerved and pale appearance told me he agreed that the obstacle at the Trap would be Spencer's *demise.*

I didn't want to think about that.

"Why would you help Spencer before yourself?"

Kace dropped his hand away from my shoulder as he smiled, "It's just a bit of fun before I go."

Kace stuck out his head towards Maybelle telling me to go back. I nodded and started my walk of fear on the wooden bridge. I used the ledge to help me balance. If I didn't hold on, I would have thought I was going to fall over. I felt dizzy as my face felt like it flushed red.

Maybelle walked towards me, her lips pursed together. Her eyes furrowed together once she got a good look at me. She barely opened her mouth when she spoke, "Mia." Maybelle looked at me again and shifted her eyebrows back to normal. "You okay?"

I nodded my head and gave her the same upturned reassuring smile Kace had given me. I then widened my smile to show my teeth. I hoped I was more genuine-looking as I fibbed, "I'm fine."

Maybelle wrapped her arm around my shoulder. The reach was perfect for her comfort. Her shoulder met my neck, so her arm wrapped comfortably against my shoulder blades. Her hand rested against the strap of my shield. My shield has been on me for days nonstop and now felt like it was a part of me. I barely noticed its existence. Maybelle paused before speaking again, waiting for us to get close to Nerissa and Lauren who were beside the boulders, "So, I have decided. We light the yearly bomb soon after Spencer leaves and then we help you. It makes sense that way."

I resisted the urge to laugh at the simplicity of her sentence. I let my top lip vibrate as I exhaled to give me something to distract me from how annoyed Maybelle's words made me feel. *It makes sense that way. It makes sense for who?*

But if the bomb lights then the challenge is over. I'd be stuck here.

I pressed my lips together and grit my teeth. I looked up at Maybelle. "If I stay after the bomb is lit, I—"

Maybelle nodded before she interrupted me, placing her draped arm back to her side. "You become a Queen. You're a Neutral so you take the place of Marissa." I looked up at the aura of smoke in front of me. It hovered gracefully above the center boulder right in front of my feet. The smoke bobbed slightly. Maybelle tilted her head to the left to look at me and shook her head. She placed her hand on my shoulder. Her grip was slightly too rough to be comfortable. I shook it off as she spoke. "I don't think she's alive anymore, Mia. You'd be perfect in her place." Maybelle turned to look at me better. One of her eyes was pink, the other a blaring red. Maybelle's eyes changing from its pale pink natural state to a darker color signaled her annoyance. It was best to stay away from her at these times. I shuddered as she spoke. "I'm going to do this for you. Do you trust me, Mia?"

There was the word again: *trust.* Maybelle's previous judgment of trusting me had shocked me. How could anyone believe in me so quickly? But now the question was whether or not I would reciprocate. Maybelle wasn't the kindest, but none of her anger has been directed towards me. She would easily get annoyed towards Nerissa and even sometimes Lauren, but never to me. We had a motherly connection. If you could even call it that. But were her actions towards me faked? Did she mean them?

I had always assumed that if everything here was possible, shouldn't reviving people be possible too? But acknowledging Kace's story there was no straightforward answer.

Could there be a possibility to get my mother back?

But, ultimately, whether or not I actually trusted her was not the issue at the moment. I had to make sure Spencer was safe. My sleeve that was once rolled up had fallen down a bit. The exposure of my skin allowed me to see one sentence. *But a final breath a boy must take.*

Final.

Final.

Final.

Final breath.

I let out a jagged breath, trying extremely hard to not

hyperventilate as my chest heaved. I let out a short soft hiccup that threatened to make the water piling up in my lower eyelid fall down.

I nodded. The left corner of Maybelle's lip twitched up in response but she wasn't smiling, it was more of a *it is what it is.* I looked down as Maybelle pressed her cold long fingers to my back to forcefully push me towards her. She gave me a firm hug. Her body was rigid and her grip was tense. I didn't put my arms around her and just stayed in her embrace. I looked up at her and she let go.

Spencer. I needed to give him a cue to attack. But how could I make eye contact with someone who is currently invisible?

Maybelle grabbed my shoulders which jolted my head forward. She hissed, "Don't look behind you." Her grip on my shoulders increased, slightly digging her long natural nails into my skin. The force of her grip knocked my shield off my shoulders. Maybelle loosened her grip so I could bend down to get it, her eyes fixated on what was behind me. Crouching down I could feel the warmth of something behind me. My assumption was confirmed as I heard a crackling sound. *Fire. Spencer.* Maybelle stepped to my left, her heeled suede boots rested in front of my shoulder. The maroon color of them was very vibrant. Looking high up to see Maybelle's arm's hurt my eyes, so I stood up, reaching for the strap of my shield. Vines wrapped around her arms. The vines were a pale green with darker leaves attached to the stems. The center of the leaves was brighter than the green surrounding them. The thorns that interchangeably were attached to the stems had a red tint to their pale green appearance. The vines bunched up together in the crevice of her elbow. The vines were wrapped around tight, but from Maybelle's facial expression and the lack of color in her arm, I could tell they didn't pain her. Maybelle gripped the ledge of the bridge as I turned over. *Spencer.* He was visible now. Spencer's fire wasn't completely activated anymore, only sparks of fire leftover from his nails. The tip of my ears heated up from the roaring crackles from Spencer's hand. Maybelle tightened her grip and the vines on her arm extended from under her short sleeves across the bridge towards Spencer. Spencer waited to see what would happen as the vines extended towards his feet. Spencer's face went pale as the fire beneath his nail beds kindled. My eyes widened as an unexpected vine pressed against his neck. Spencer knelt forward, unable to keep his hands aflame. He let out a soft, raspy cough.

"Maybelle," I hissed at the woman next to me. When I leaned towards her, her hair blew in my face. Blonde strands traveled near my eyes. I blinked and brushed them off and in the process pushed my coils of hair to the increasing sweat on my face. My hand flew towards my hip, curling my fingers over a blade that rested on my belt. I took a second to get the dagger comfortably in my hand. I could feel every ingrained crevice of detail on it: the embellishments of red glassy hearts that repeated down the handle and the carved out flower pattern. The curved-shaped handle suited my small and stubby hands perfectly. *I love this dagger.* I shook my head to get myself to focus. Maybelle stayed in her same position as more vines went around Spencer's neck as he tried to get his hand under them so the sharpness of the vines wouldn't touch his throat. I looked down at Maybelle's annoyingly soft-looking shoes. I slammed the dagger into her shoe, hoping to not cut one of her toes. Maybelle slid her hand off the ledge as she turned towards me.

I turned away from her, looking at Spencer. The green to his eyes was dimmed from the lighting.

"Now," I breathed out. With the lack of Maybelle's control, the vines went limp. Spencer rubbed at his nails a couple of times, vainly trying to get his fire to spark. He groaned before rubbing it against the vine near his hand. The plant caught on fire. The stem blackened as the crimson color rested on the plant.

The rest of the plant caught on fire. Blackened leaves crumbled before my feet. The fire grew.

I did not like fire.

I scrambled backward, bringing my shield to my face. *Thank God for this shield.* The sense of familiarity with the shield provided me relief. I pressed the tips of my fingers against the gold embellished intricate design around the center of the shield. The outer rim had neatly designed flowers, buds, and vines that were carved in. Pressing my fingers on the bumps of the design, I could feel the floral pattern imprinting on my hand. My right hand rested on the design of a budding rose that was about to bloom and my left hand rested on a constructed embellishment of a hand pulling on some of the vines that were carved out. The design on the shield was beautiful; a piece of art versus a weapon. The center of the shield had dark planks of mahogany wood. And carved out of the wood was the not equal to sign which was what I was told to be the sign of someone who is a Neutral.

The fire spread, causing me to step back even further. I dropped the shield. The fire was too low to block me from the fire with it anyway. I rubbed at the newfound marks on my fingertips. I could feel the curve of my heel press down on the hard surface of the bridge. The feel of wind against the heel of my foot that hung off the pier startled me before I felt the rush of the air press me down. I held my breath quickly, expecting to fall into the sea. The coolness of water froze my face up. I reached for the blurry pier I had just fallen off from. The smell of salt from the water that was up my nose made me feel nauseous. I could tell from the loud sound of water blocking out the distant voices on top of me that I had the salty water up my ears too. A scaly fin pressed against my foot. I kicked my foot away, not worried about what touched me, in a haste to get to the pier before the very little amount of oxygen I had was sucked out of my lungs. My eyes stung from the saltiness of the water. The water wasn't clean, making my efforts to see the bridge harder. The pier was barely visible, just another shade of green-blue in the vast amount of water I was under. I resisted the urge to scream from the lack of income of oxygen as something scaly wrapped around my foot. My soul seemed to leave my body as the force of the scales yanked me down. Bubbles, from air escaping my nose and from the force of my body sinking, spread around me, making it incredibly hard to see. I struggled to keep my eyes open, the stinging feeling shifting into a burning sensation.

Remembering Kace's story, I smiled. *I'm going to be fine.*

Chapter Twenty-three

Never mind

There was now a searing pain in my eyes. Each time I blinked the pain got even worse. My leg was very uncomfortable from the feel of something scaly moving around it, but I wasn't worried about that: I needed to get to air fast. My lungs heaved trying to exhale, but I forced the uncomfortable feeling down. My face was burning up as much as my eyes from the lack of oxygen.

The problem with my water manipulation was that I couldn't create water. It's impossible to control something that wasn't there and I couldn't control it when I was under a cumbersome amount of it. It would have been helpful to know the second part beforehand; the feeling of uselessness while you sink wasn't the most pleasant.

Fire manipulation had its benefits. People with fire manipulation were able to use the heat of their blood to warm it more to create a fiery substance. According to Kace, when people with fire abilities are modified when coded, a level of alcohol is added to their bloodstream to spark the flames (Kace had a pyromaniac-like fascination with fire, managing to deliberately share every fact he knew about spontaneous human combustion as I cringed away in horror. I had a feeling Spencer and Kace would get along because of their similar interest in flames).

Maybelle's ability also didn't allow for the creation of something that wasn't there. She wore a sheet of leaves and vines under her clothing for her use to work at any time. As a Neutral, I had access to all of these powers, however, fire and plants had no use for me underwater. In addition, it seemed like my teleportation skills didn't work underwater either, as I recalled the first time I tried to teleport. I winced remembering my fall from the bridge.

I yanked my foot away from the living thing pushing me under. A pair of round yellow eyes with weaved in amber irises scared the hell out of me as the leftover air in my expanded cheeks threatened to push out. The water around the creature glowed blue to match its iridescent indigo scales. There was nothing largely threatening about the creature besides its curled in thin lips that extended all the way to the sides of its face. It oddly looked as if it was grinning. The adrenaline pumping in my body also could have been because of the fact that I've never seen this type of creature before. From its glow in its bright scales to the round red plates following the curvature of the creature's back the entire animal was something extremely unique. There was only one creature that this animal could be: *Rose.* Kace's drawing was a masterpiece and I stood in awe of his creation. I squeezed my eyes shut to help me remember Kace's story. *Design an obstacle only Neutrals can control.* I could control Rose, but *how?*

Not wanting to breathe out, I realized it would be a hassle to verbally speak to Rose. My first reaction was to dramatically gesture actions that I wanted Rose to do. I first pointed at it, then above us, and finally tried to mimic what I wanted it to do. Rose cocked its head to the left in confusion. I groaned. I took all the strength I had to speak in as few words as possible. Rose seemed to comprehend and used her snout to push me up. It swam to my left as

I hastily grabbed the edge of the pier in vain. The edge of the bridge was slippery and hard to grab. I reached up again, sinking my nails into the crevices of the damp wood. The feel of air in my lungs wasn't as pleasant as I thought; the newfound oxygen burned in my lungs. There was some salty water drying out my throat and I forcefully coughed it out. I had no strength and no motivation to pull myself up. A splash of water tickled my nose as the stillness of the water was brashly disturbed by Rose arising from the water. Rose's slits for nostrils flared as its gills closed up at the change of incoming oxygen. Its lips curved in even more as it bore its sharp canines. The plan was in action and Rose understood what I wanted it to do. Holding myself up was becoming harder as I focused on what Rose was about to do. I heaved myself up just enough for me to rest my arms on the ledge.

Rose went to Maybelle first, but Maybelle was prepared. Maybelle clenched her fists to gain access to her nature ability but Rose moved to the other side of her. Before even I was prepared, the creature sunk its canines into Maybelle's shoulder. She howled and it pained my ears. I looked away. Rose moved in front of me to witness Lauren who was to my right. I looked back at Maybelle who had now collapsed seemingly lifeless on the bridge. It was a good thing everyone was immortal during the High Tide Challenge and Maybelle had extra protection because, as a Queen, she was immortal in general as long as she was in High Tide. But with a near-death experience, it seemed to take time before her wound healed. I inhaled to dive myself back into the water, still using my fingers to clutch the pier's ledge so that I didn't have to watch the same thing happen to Lauren. At the sound of a shriek, I pulled myself up again.

My hair was completely drenched now. My hair was on the denser side and each strand was coated in droplets of water. My head felt as though it was weighing me down. I would kill for a hair tie. Some strands stuck to my forehead and I noticed clear drops of water falling down onto my nose. I dug my fingers into the bridge in an effort to get more grip to hoist myself up. I could feel myself slipping down the pier again. The infiltration of a copper-like smell filled my nose. I scrunched my nose in disgust. Rose had now rolled over, resting on the bridge to ask Nerissa to give it a belly rub. Nerissa was seemingly cautious at first before hesitantly deciding to place her hand on the scales of Rose's stomach. Rose wriggled closer to the lady while wagging its tail as if it were programmed to be a dog.

A pair of soaked, black Converse shoes were placed in front of me. The laces were slightly pulled apart and the tips were drenched from the pool of water in front of my arms. The shoes were recognizable and I recalled them to be Spencer's. One of his pant legs was slightly rolled up while the other stayed down. His shirt was tucked in his pants to cover up the fact that his shirt was imprinted with wrinkles. His hair wasn't much more organized; some of his strands near where he parted his hair stuck up against gravity.

"Help me up," I rasped. Spencer continued to stare at me.

Spencer crouched down, pulling my arm a bit so it rested more comfortably on the wood of the bridge. He opened his mouth to speak. "You can't live like this."

I wrinkled the skin between my eyebrows before responding, "Okay? And what does that have to do with you helping me?" I heaved my body up so that both of my arms were comfortably on the wood of the bridge. The hairs on my arms stood up, causing bumps on my forearms. The water was warmer than land and the feel of High Tide's cool breeze made me shiver.

To my surprise he used the tips of his fingers to pull himself up, bouncing on the balls of his feet. He now seemed to tower over me, his hands that could have pulled me up were too far to reach. He lifted his right hand slightly above his ear as he dropped his head slightly as a sign of protest. "You left me first," he reminded me. I was shockingly reminded of the time I tried to convince him to use the Trap, and the time I left him to go to the Tech building. I cringed at both events.

I never would have taken him as a revenge seeker, but that was the only way I could describe him now. But his choice of words stumped me. Spencer wasn't known for spitting words around and always thought before he spoke. *You can't live like this.* What did he mean by that? Did he think it was wrong that I was associating with Maybelle or did he think my personality had changed? Or was it something else entirely? As much as I didn't want to waste my time thinking about him while I participated in the High Tide Challenge, I, for some reason, still cared what he thought of me.

The Trap. You need to remind Spencer not to leave.

With sudden motivation, I forced my feet onto the bridge. A feeling of nausea swarmed my senses. I took a wobbly step forward.

"Spencer! Wait!" I called out. But it was too late. He was too far away to hear me.

Final breath.

Chapter Twenty-four

USB #1

It's been a few months and it felt as if time was my enemy. As each month passed, I'd hope that the challenge would end.

Living here was sickening. Every few days another one of Kace's creatures would require a fight. My whole body ached, despite my skin being clear of any damage.

But for the game to even end would require Spencer to either escape or die in High Tide. I didn't want either to happen.

I haven't even seen Spencer since he conflicted with Maybelle. No one has seen him. The one thing I've learned about Spencer here is that he's good at hiding.

I was fighting twice as many creatures as I was supposed to since none of them were able to even find Spencer.

I stuck the dagger I was twirling in my hands into the sand.

This side of the sea was more peaceful with the lack of Maybelle's presence. The woods and the building where I discovered Lauren's prophecy were behind me. I wondered if I could see trees like this on Earth. The trees were tall, but their branches hung down with wide, flat leaves. It was ironic that the woods were labeled Dangerous Area Woods.

I dug my feet into the sand, taking in the scenery around

me. I loved this area and that's why I continued to tell Kace to meet me here.

"Mia."

I looked up at Kace who was bending down to sit beside me. I cocked my head at the white box in his hands.

"What's in that?"

"I brought you clothes," he smiled. "You've been wearing those this entire time, so I decided you should be able to get the same privileges I have and be able to change."

I looked at him skeptically. "Why are you being so nice to me?"

"I'm sorry?" He questioned.

"You started off being so pissy to me and now after a few weeks of meeting me here, you've lost your sarcastic nature," I clarified.

He looked down while speaking to me. "Well, I guess I've gotten used to you."

I shrugged at his answer, opening the box he gave me. A pair of white work pants caught my eye. I pushed it off to reveal a muscle tank top. I rubbed the fabric in between my fingers. The clothes were soft and *clean.*

Being away from your house for a while is bound to create homesickness, which is exactly what the High Tide Challenge provoked. There was nothing worse than feeling uncomfortable in your filth without the ability to scrub it off within the comfort of your own home.

The clothes Kace gave me made me hyperaware of the dirt on my body. I shivered in disgust.

I took a breath out before turning to Kace. "Thank you," I said and smiled as I looked down at the clothes. The clothes were all white. "How fast do you think I'd get them dirty?"

He huffed in amusement, "You can thank Lauren for that."

I laughed before changing the conversation. "Okay, so if you could wear any other color, what would you wear?"

He contemplated this before opening his mouth. "I think I like white on me. Wouldn't you agree that I look amazing in these clothes?"

"Sure, but it's *boring* now."

"I don't know. I don't like to stand out," he admitted.

"You don't like to stand out because you're afraid of what other people's opinions of you are. That's why you're so cold all the time," I realized.

Kace huffed in disbelief. "Do you always psychoanalyze people?"

"I am not *psychoanalyzing* you!" I exclaimed. "I'm just trying to understand you. You and Spencer are basically the same person. You two get afraid when someone tries to get close to you."

Kace looked up at me with a sense of insecurity. He was using self-comforting methods: with his arms crossed, his hands rubbed his neck. "Why does Spencer hate me?" Kace asked quietly.

There were no denying Spencer's hateful looks and sharp remarks at Kace, but childishly I didn't want Kace to feel hurt. "He doesn't hate you," I lied.

With a more assertive tone, Kace interrupted me, "Yes, he does." He calmed himself by taking a deep breath in before bitterly pitying himself. "He hates that I'm not as smart as him. He thinks I'm stupid.

I protested. "He doesn't hate you!" It sounded like I was trying to convince myself. I really hated comforting people. I never knew what to say. I cringed at my words. I sounded so passive.

"It's okay, Mia. The truth doesn't hurt me."

"But you look hurt," I somberly remarked. "You're not stupid, Kace."

Kace refused to look me in the eyes. "Okay."

Feeling the need to distract himself, Kace reached for my

dagger that was still in the sand. I flinched. Kace noticed me and looked at me, concerned.

"Did you think I was going to attack you?" he accused me, looking hurt.

I looked away from him.

"I wouldn't hurt you." He paused, waiting for me to say something. My silence made him turn red in anger. "You know I wouldn't hurt you, right?"

I crossed my arms. "You already hurt me indirectly." I sucked a breath in and continued. "But it's your job though, so I shouldn't blame you." I stood up with Kace's box in my hands. "Thanks for the clothes."

Kace didn't look back to call for me; his eyes still facing forward as he spoke, "Mia."

I walked forward tentatively. Kace pulled out my dagger brashly, the sand mound that the dagger was placed in collapsing. My breath quickened, but all Kace did was gently hand me back my dagger. Despite my visible fear, Kace calmly reached into his pocket. He stared at the USB that was taken out of his pocket before extending his arm forward so that I could clearly see it.

"What is that?" I asked confusedly.

"All the creatures I made that were specifically supposed to attack you have been removed from my computers and put into this USB," Kace asserted.

Kace threw the USB up and I watched as it fell down on his palm before he chucked it into the blue mass in front of us.

Relief came over me as I heard the dainty splash the USB made as it sunk into the water.

Chapter Twenty-five

Courtney

Today was the day I decided that I thought that wet sand was disgusting (not that I knew exactly what *today* meant; I had completely lost track of time, more worried about the High Tide Challenge than anything else; but I was sure if I asked Spencer he would know). I stared at my hand that now had a pile of damp sand in it. Granulated particles of the sand that didn't soak up the water scratched the palm of my hand and I glared at it. It didn't help that there was an obnoxious thumping above me. I looked up and quickly pivoted away from another chunk of sand that splat onto the ground beside me. I sat beside the sea on the rocky, off-white sand. I scrunched my nose as I looked at my occupied left hand and turned it to watch the blob of sand drop right beside my feet. My toes were dug into the nice *dry* sand. It wasn't weird that sand was falling from the sky since we were underground, however it was strange that I was able to hear noises from above me.

I heard the thump again. My toes twitched. *Maybe it's from below.*

I felt the need to investigate after I got the sand off my body. I kept my sand-covered left hand away from my body as I shook my foot in a poor attempt to brush some of the sand off. I hobbled to the gushing water that soaked the sand near it. I walked in so that my feet would be covered by the cool substance. I bent over to cup some of the cold water in my palms and rubbed it against the sand particles lodged in my skin. I noticed the tips of my pants were saturated by the water and I rolled them up to my thighs before walking over to the bridge to my left. I placed my feet in between the openings on either side of the poles that reached up to the railings of the bridge. I took my right foot to swing it across the railing to support my left leg as I pulled it away from the water to stand on the bridge. I stepped into my shoes, pushing my socks to the side of the bridge since I was too lazy to attempt to slide them on my damp feet. I wiggled my feet so that my toes were placed comfortably against the broken-down curve of my shoe. I reached for my dagger and slid it through the pouch on the middle of my shield. I slung the shield's chain over my shoulder and looked up to clearly see the falling sand in front of me.

Sand was falling, but it wasn't from a force from above me. The ground below me appeared to shake. A rattling sound from a section where the sand met the brick ground shook in my ears. It seemed as though the two were pulling away from each other.

I walked forward. My feet pressed down against the hot sand every time I took a step. The noise led me to a familiar area. I walked forward, not looking under me. My chest dropped as I felt an area where the ground wasn't support-ing my foot. The sound of my fall rang through my ears. My jaw clenched as I tentatively reached for my left arm which took the impact of my fall. I winced as my fingers brushed my skin.

"Are you okay?" a feminine voice asked. "Here, come in." Light from an object shone through the darkness. Being a left-handed person, I used the hand that I fell on to try to get up. In pain, I collapsed back to the hard, cold ground. Even though broken bones heal in High, the pain always lingers.

The girl's strong grip pulled me up. Her orange eyes filled the area, glowing. They weren't a neon orange, but a dark and somehow-glowing orange. I wasn't surprised about the abnormality of her eyes since modifications existed here, but it confused me that out of all colors someone would choose the one she had.

Using her flashlight, the girl guided me to a rusted metal door. She fished for something in her pocket and used it to unlock the door. The door squeaked as she opened it. I stared at the intricate, flowy design on the key. Each swirl and curve led to one small hole on the top, allowing it to be hooked on a key chain if needed be. The girl slammed the door shut the moment I walked in, leaving the patterned key in the keyhole.

I wanted to tell her that she forgot her key, but my mouth felt too dry to open.

I looked to the doorway in front of us. A sign with the glowing letters "E-X-I-T" hung above it.

I chewed my lip. Escaping couldn't be that easy.

I remember Maybelle telling me about her deliberate plan to block the exits. I never really listened to what she said; her rants seemed endless, but I remembered one thing: she couldn't block out one exit. The Trap.

I recalled what Kace said about a one-of-a-kind monster guarding it. I looked over at the girl next to me.

Could a human be one of Kace's Tech-modified monsters?

"Courtney," the girl greeted me by sticking her hand out.

"Mi—" I took her hand before I spoke.

"Mia, I know." Courtney's hand led up to my hair, her fingers getting caught up in knots in my split ends. I inched away; I hated when other people touched my hair without my permission. "You know, the last time I saw you, you had auburn hair. Now it's a dark brown. Did you dye it?"

"No, it has always been this way," I softly muttered. "How do you know me?"

"Of course, you don't remember me," Courtney said plainly with sadness hinted in her voice. "You were too young."

"I don't remember anything before second grade," I confessed.

"That's right. The fire." Courtney divulged. I tensed up and Courtney pulled her hand out of my curly locks. I grabbed my hair out of pain. After Courtney spoke again. "Sorry, I didn't want to—"

"I'm fine," I irked speedily. I was curious now. "Did you know me before you got here? How did you get here?"

My mind buzzed. *If this girl knows me I need to know more about her.*

Luckily, this time I didn't have to pry as I did with Kace. "Sit down," Courtney said, then gestured to the metal bed with balled-up fuzzy polyester and cotton sheets in the room. "I'll tell you my story." Hesitating, I sat down. Courtney sat down beside me.

Chapter Twenty-six

It Was Her Brother

Courtney sprang up, breathing heavily. Another nightmare. Courtney Ivy Meyer lives underground. And no, she doesn't like it. Her room is a metal box with a rusting metal bed. Not much to describe besides the natural glow that silver metal had. The room was simply boring. It contained walls, a bed, a lame inadequate blanket (that was, in fact, the only thing not made of metal, by the way), and a rectangle LED light that flickered every two seconds. It was like an underground jail cell made out of metal. Well, it was a jail cell. It was named High Tide Detainment for a reason. Each person here was convicted of a crime in High Tide, which was stupid because High Tide had no clear-cut laws. But when you burn down half of its civilization, you'd assume they'd want to keep you detained. There was also some sort of hesitation towards the use of fire on High Tide as Courtney recalled Maybelle's uncomfortable expression as she ushered Courtney to the High Tide Police.

Besides the extreme plainness of the room, however, there was something special about it: a worn-down elevator. Courtney eyed it with curiosity. The more she squinted at it, the more she got annoyed that she couldn't go in it. She eyed the padlock. She looked over to her right. The door keeping her from freedom was bolted shut. Only those from outside could open the door.

Courtney huffed as she recalled what got her here in the first place. The more she thought about it, the more she got annoyed, for it wasn't Courtney's fault that she ended up here. It was her brother's. Her eyes furrowed at the thought of her brother. She could make out each of his features despite not seeing him in years. She smiled at the thought of his childish round cheeks, the rosiness to his fingers, the warm tone to his face and hair, and the way his golden hair stuck out in different directions. Because although there was no forgiving what her brother did, he was still a tiny child and she loved him.

However, the happy memories were quick to fade. Courtney wrapped her arms around her knees as flashbacks of the event pierced her mind.

The place was lit with gleaming lights that you didn't want to see. My brother's eyes were wide open in horror.

"Courtney did it!"

Yeah, I'm the older sister. Blame it on me, Courtney's thoughts grimaced. There was one thing she knew for sure: she was a High Tide Competitor too. She had fire abilities.

Turns out the day her brother blamed things on Courtney Ivy Meyer, her brother had lit anywhere matches. Dumb, she knows. Hey, he was the one who said to strike them on her hands! That's when she got the realization that she had the same abilities as some of the kids who were able to participate in the High Tide Challenge. It pained her that she couldn't compete herself. All because of her dumb brother and her parents who brought her here.

Her parents were former High Tide Techs, relieved of their positions. But there was something magical about being a Tech that Courtney's parents admired and still valued. They dreamed of coming back. And so both Courtney and her sibling were brought there. Courtney despised her parents for letting the officers put her in detainment. They could have bailed her out, but they choose not to. Why?

Courtney is not the only kid in the friendly dorm suite. If stereotypes were real, her friend (well he thought Courtney was his friend at least), Andrew would be the troublemaker: shitty personality, edgy style, and of course the needed thoughtless and spontaneous spunk every troublemaker had. Andrew oddly reminded Courtney of her brother with their matching lack of street smarts. Not that Courtney was much smarter, but that was beside the point. Besides she was bullied enough for being the stereotype of the dumb blonde. But it seems as though two stereotypes attract.

There was nothing attractive about Andrew, well according to Courtney's opinion. He had average blue eyes, an average masculine-like square face, and average brown hair that was oftentimes greasy because of his unhygienic lack of showers. There were some unconventional features to Andrew as well: the small mole to the left of his mouth and his hooked nose. There wasn't anything inherently interesting about Andrew, certainly not his personality. As much as Andrew would like to believe he was humorous, he just wasn't able to keep up a conversation. Courtney quickly grew tired of his short remarks. Courtney quickly grew tired of her acquaintance in general.

On top of that, they were both stuck in the same building. However, Andrew had been here way longer than Courtney and was almost an adult now, being at the ripe old age of seventeen. So long he could almost laugh about it, but we all know High Tide isn't a laughing matter. It's a death trap. Or a death wait if you were in detainment too.

Chapter Twenty-seven

There Is a Reason Why People Don't Go In Broken Elevators

It was fun. It was fun watching the padlock burn. There was an elastic quality to it when it heated up and it was easy for Courtney to loosen the lock to pull it away from the handle. The transfer of warmth from the padlock to her hand was calming. Not that Courtney would try to use it anyway. The air had the lingering smell of smoke which the teen loved. It also had a scent that Courtney had never smelled before. The smell of metal molting.

There wasn't much in the room to practice her fire manipulation. She needed the bed and the blanket, and wouldn't dare to burn such necessities. The clock was somewhat important even though she couldn't care less about what time it was, but she decided that she didn't want to burn that object either. If she burned the walls, the police would be sure to notice and she didn't want to get into trouble. Burning something living was sometimes an option. Rats would often crawl through openings in her room she couldn't even see and occasionally she'd fall into the temptation of burning one (and she could always burn Andrew, not that she ever would, but the temptation was still there sometimes). There were no rats in her room, but her desire to light something on fire was still present. There was one thing she could burn: the padlock. She was sure of the fact that if she never entered the inside of the elevator again, the police officers wouldn't even notice the missing padlock if they ever felt the need to look through her room.

Besides she did notice the Out of Order sign and took it as a warning to not touch the handle again. Although living in a metal box had no entertainment factors, she wasn't ready to die yet and especially not because of a broken elevator.

Courtney crouched down to slide the contorted lock under the bed as she heard the creak of her door opening. She shrieked, hitting her head on the top of the bed.

"Calm down. It's me," a familiar voice spoke. Courtney slid her head away from the bed frame after tucking the lock between unpleasant piles of dust bunnies under her bed and rubbed at her neck as Andrew spoke again. "I tried opening that elevator door yesterday. Do you think you can pull the lock apart with your ability?"

How ironic.

Andrew pressed the plastic button for the elevator door to slide open as Courtney absentmindedly tried to wipe the remaining dust on her fingers onto her pants.

"Did you not notice the out-of-order sign?" Courtney pointed to the top of the elevator as Andrew looked to his left to examine the plastic handle. He snorted and pointed to the lack of a padlock securing the case covering the button that started the elevator.

Courtney growled at him, "It's out of order for a reason. I didn't try to go in it."

Andrew furrowed his eyebrows as he repositioned his black sweater. "Then why did the button work?" Andrew pointed to the plastic button he had just pressed down.

The two doors creaked as they pulled away from each other. Andrew noticed Courtney's wariness of the unsteadiness of the doors and continued, "Let's check the handle." The elevator worked by twisting the handle in a circular motion to guide the elevator down. Andrew paused before stepping into the elevator. It didn't wobble and seemed stable enough. Andrew pointed out the handle to Courtney before tentatively touching the handle. Andrew spun the handle one rotation. The elevator went down a foot. Courtney couldn't see Andrew's feet anymore. Andrew shrugged his shoulders. "Everything seems to be working."

Courtney exhaled, "If you fall to your death, it's not my fault."

"No," Andrew said as he stepped out from the elevator, "It wouldn't be because you'd fall to your death too."

Andrew reached for Courtney's wrist. She pulled it away. Courtney glared at Andrew as he looked at her to see if she wanted to come or not. Courtney let out an angry sigh and stood up.

"This is a dumb idea, but—" Courtney paused to look at Andrew, whose right foot was already in the elevator. Courtney raised her eyebrows. "Fine, I'll come with you."

Andrew smiled and stood properly in the elevator as he waited for Courtney to enter. Andrew slammed his hand against Courtney's back to appreciate her agreement. Courtney clenched her fists to threaten Andrew to not do that again as he laughed and pushed the handle down and back up again.

The lower they went, the darker it became. Courtney's feet tingled at the impact of the elevator hitting something hard. The elevator door opened but it wasn't much brighter outside.

Andrew felt around for a wall as Courtney's pupils grew. Instead of black, everything was a dark gray. She could finally see Andrew now, who looked like a dark blob. "A door!" he exclaimed, his hand resting on something solid.

"Andrew," Courtney scolded. The elevator might have been safe, but there was no telling what would be behind that door.

"Come on! It's safe and there's light!" he said as he peeked his head through the doorway.

When they walked through, the light blinded Courtney for a moment. The area was lit with a purple-bluish glow with a red fog. Where has she seen this before? And then the realization hit her. It was High Tide.

"I'm leaving!" Courtney exclaimed, throwing her hands in the air while turning towards the door behind her.

Andrew rolled his eyes, then followed her to the door. It was dark again. Andrew grabbed Courtney's hand and dragged her to the door. This was what Courtney always wanted, so why was she walking away from it? All she wanted was to compete in the High Tide Challenge and become a Queen. Courtney pulled her hand away from Andrew and stared at the door. This was it. And she was walking away from it.

The thing with fear is that it stops us. And it sure stopped Courtney that day. The salty smell of the air and the hazy look of the sky weren't new feelings. She recognized that place: the setting her nightmares had and the day she was sent here. As much as she wanted to walk through the opening, she couldn't.

There was something safe and peaceful about her jail cell, so there was no doubt in her mind when she vowed to never spin the handle again.

Okay, fine. Maybe there was a little doubt. But definitely not enough for Courtney to want to go back.

Chapter Twenty-eight

Tick, Tock

"That story is fake," I remarked. There were some obvious factual pieces, like the existence of Andrew (there was an obnoxious sound of a man snoring obliviously nearby. I wrinkled my nose. Men never ceased to disgust me) and it made sense that her parents didn't bail her out because they were Techs and they modified her to harm anyone who entered the Trap. She was a High Tide Obstacle after all; she was designed by her parents to be detrimental to Competitors like me who wanted to escape. However, there was one part of the story that didn't sit right with me. Courtney didn't strike me to be a scared person. She evidently was vicious in some sort of way because how else could no one escape from the Trap? I shivered at the thought that my grandpa was found dead outside the Trap. There was an incomprehensible nature to her actions in the story. I couldn't understand anyone who didn't put in the effort to achieve what they wanted. *How could Courtney just walk away? She was so close.*

It also unsettled me that she thought she knew me. I was sure I'd recognize someone like Courtney in my life.

Kace's computer contained information on everyone in High Tide. As one of his monsters, I wondered if Courtney had access to it.

Courtney furrowed her eyebrows. "Excuse me?"

I had a continuous feeling that Courtney's story had been modified by Kace or some other Tech. She had shared her story effortlessly without any bumps of needing to recall anything.

Kace took time to pause and explain the story of how he got to High Tide, and his arrival a couple of years ago. Courtney, on the other hand, made no pauses and easily remembered parts of her life that happened when she was younger.

"How long have you been here?" I quietly asked, hoping the change would distract her from my past words.

Courtney slowly relaxed her face before she responded. "Years. Almost as long as I remember."

That explained it. Everything she remembered was because of her modification. Everything she was able to reflect on was too long ago for a human to recall. If she couldn't remember the exact year of her detainment, how could she recall even smaller details of her past?

"Well, anyway, thanks for sharing your story with me." I had the sudden urge to get out of the room. Nothing was comforting about sitting in a box made of metal and Courtney didn't make the situation more pleasant either.

The Queens of High Tide never felt human-like with their modified immortality and large and threatening auras. They carried themselves like whiny Greek gods and that's how they appeared. Even with their personality imperfections, they were completely perfect.

Spencer and Kace were no different. They both had a sense of mental agility that I could never reach. They seemed untouchable, unreachable.

Spencer with his intelligence and Eurocentric features was something I wanted but never could understand. I used to have a feeling of jealousy when I met him; jealous about how, although he was mixed, he looked like the standards everyone wanted. He acted the standard too, putting a polite face in front of everyone.

And Kace with his beauty in creativity and wits made me long for his talents in awe. His creativity was on a higher level than others, being able to create something innovative in seconds.

But the same couldn't be said about Courtney. Even while knowing she was modified in some way, she seemed so utterly human and fragile. Her eyes were slanted differently than anyone else, her unconventional nose curved at the bridge, her hair laid stringy and lifeless, her bones jut out from her wrist and fingers, her face had a tint of red to it, matching the shade on her bony knuckles. Spencer and Kace seemed like a different species compared to Courtney. She seemed so perishable, but there was something beautiful about it.

See, the thing with familiarity is that it's just as scary as something new. Courtney understood what it was like to be different from others, to contain her fiery personality from others. It terrified me to see someone as raw and unnerved as me.

But like me, she had met Spencer before. Courtney had come in contact with his ability to use his intellect to be charming and personable. And also like me, Courtney would likely listen to whatever he said in a heartbeat. Spencer had a style of communication that was clear, concise, and forced you to listen to him. It worked with me; I was easily convinced. But there was no doubt in my mind that Courtney would be as susceptible if Spencer ever wanted to use her to escape from the Trap.

"No problem." Courtney wrapped her fragile arms around my neck and squeezed me close to her. The itchy fabric of her puffy purple shirt scratched my shoulders. I shrugged away from her, uncomfortable from the sudden embrace.

Her skin was abnormally cold and it made the situation even more unpleasant.

I had to admit: something was intriguing about her, despite the awkward hug, getting to know her as a friend seemed like a fantasy. She was upbeat and sometimes sarcastic when she was entertaining me with her story. Courtney was lively and unmatched, but it pained me that she was supposed to be someone I was supposed to compete against, being one of Kace's creations. I could never see who she actually was beneath all the Tech modifications she had gone through.

Courtney's broad smile disappeared; she started to have a more serious tone. "I met your friend. I can help him escape if you want. Spence is his name, right?" I winced at Spencer's name. The thing that pained me the most was that she used my nickname for Spencer. Did she know him that well that she'd call him that or was that her modification of manipulation talking?

You can't trust her. The Techs are trying to get to you. Wasn't she supposed to make sure no one escapes from the Trap? What is going on?

I paused. I played back her sentence in my head. *Spence is his name.* The only Tech that was near me when I addressed Spencer by his nickname was Kace. My blood boiled. How could he code that into Courtney? I looked down at my nails that were once painted white by Kace. I thought he genuinely cared about me.

But what upset me even more was the task at hand. I couldn't let Courtney think that Spencer was willing to go back home.

"He'll be fine. He doesn't need to escape."

"If you say so."

Courtney took a deep breath in and turned to smile at me. She then shrugged. "If he stays long enough after the competition, he automatically becomes a King. What Queen do you think he'd replace? Allison or Nerissa?" My eyes widened at Nerissa's name. How would Courtney know that Nerissa was related to Spencer if she had never left the Trap? How much information were the Techs feeding into her?

More importantly: did I want Spencer to be a King? I sure as hell did not want to be a Queen, but I'd do anything to get my mother back. Would Spencer force himself to be a King to value his life? Did he have some desire to be a King?

Will he abide?

It annoyed me that the prophecy ended with a question. Did that mean he'll die regardless of if he listens to Courtney or not? Or did that mean that there was a chance he could live? I prayed that it was the latter.

I pushed myself off the metal bed using my fingers. "I better get going. Thanks for having me," I remarked, ready to get out of the stuffy room.

"I'll see you soon, Mia." Courtney stared at me, shocked at my abrupt desire to leave.

I forced a smile. "Maybe so."

Although Courtney scared me, she had some sort of effect on me. I couldn't blame her for being modified by Techs and she seemed genuinely sweet. I turned around towards her to smile at her again, genuinely this time. She hesitantly smiled back before wiggling her fingers to wave goodbye to me.

Courtney's stare continued to linger as I walked towards the door.

The sound from the clock ticking in her room rang in my ears. The sound of the contained air in the room, the vibrations from the elevator, and the thumping from the clock seemed to be more audible since neither of us was speaking.

I looked back at Courtney, whose mouth was slightly ajar as if she was contemplating saying something. Finally, she said something audible. "Mia, do you mind leaving the door slightly open?"

That was right; she couldn't open the door herself. Although I couldn't see any potential harm in letting her out, there was a gut feeling that told me to keep her contained. However, there were benefits to letting her out; she wouldn't be able to guard the opening to Earth and that would benefit future competitors. If I let her out, it would be easier for Spencer to escape, but it was likely that Courtney would help him anyway.

I looked over from the door to Courtney. My hand clasped over the door handle and I pulled it towards me. I heard the sound of the side of the door colliding with the doorway with a click.

I stared at the metal door for a few seconds before turning away.

Besides, she had the elevator if she genuinely wanted to leave. This had to be some sort of test to see if she could trust me, but if I didn't trust her why should she trust me?

I felt the feel of soft grass through the soles of my feet. I wiggled my toes as I took a breath of fresh air. It was relieving to not be in a contained area anymore.

I let another cleansing breath in and I thought of what to do next as I stared at my hand. I looked at the prophecy again. I frowned. There was an increase in determination in me.

Courtney may have never been on my side since she wanted Spencer to escape for some reason, but I had something stronger than her modification. I was a Neutral. I could do anything I needed to do.

Unlike other obstacles, Courtney wasn't created to only contain competitors in High Tide. She was also designed to kill them off, and she wouldn't stop with Spencer, even if that meant she had to let him escape.

But someone made her a monster. And I knew exactly who was maintaining her demeanor.

Kace Striker.

Chapter Twenty-nine

December First

Only one computer was turned on in the room. The screen displayed the date: December 1st. In a month another year would have passed. I longed for my time on Earth. *How long would I be stuck here?*

My nostalgia was cut short when he noticed me. The guy spun his chair so he was facing towards me. He seemed different, scary even. He leaned over, his back no longer resting against his chair. His legs were crossed and his hands were hanging over his thighs.

The screen flickered before showing the feed from the security cameras around High Tide. In a flash I was there.

Nerissa never started conversations, only speaking once spoken to. Although she was very talkative when asked something, she was quiet the majority of the time. Almost as if she had something to say constantly, but only let it out once someone else spoke to her.

Nerissa held eye contact with me as she pointed to the paddle brush in her hand and raised her eyebrows. I shrugged then nodded. I might as well have someone brush the mess of my hair.

I dipped the tips of my shoes into the still water. Rings of moving water dispersed from my feet. The wood under me felt slightly damp and the metal behind my thighs was hard and cold. The hair on the back of my neck stayed alert as Nerissa sat down behind me. She leaned forward, her short hair brushing the side of my neck. She slightly dipped the thistles of the brush into the cool water. She tapped the excess water off the brush against the side of the bridge. With her left hand, she guided the tips of my hair between her fingers. Her fingers caught onto a knot in my hair, but she didn't tug to pull it apart. She gently took the brush and pressed the thistles down on my hair. She started from the tips of my hair and worked her way up.

I had little memory of my mom trying to braid little six-year-old Mia's hair, but I remembered the braids turned out terrible. It might have been because I was an impatient child and my mom always had something to do for her job. I remembered that my mom's hair was always perfect. Her hair had barely any fly-aways and was weaved in with blonde hair which opposed her naturally dark hair.

Elaine didn't know how to take care of my hair either. She had no idea what she was doing, having never dealt with curly-haired children. Elaine opted for a high-heat straightener and a brash effort to try and flatten my hair to a point where she could easily pull a comb through it. But I didn't like waiting for my hair to be straightened completely and my hair always managed to be wavy again the next day. I stopped having Elaine do my hair and usually didn't bother to brush through my hair daily. My hair never looked the way I wanted it to anyway, with or without effort. It usually looked lifeless and the coils of my hair often stuck together. I used to look at images of curly-haired girls, wishing that my hair would be poofy and soft.

Girls at school would complain about having straight hair. I loved the appearance of having curly hair, but I just didn't want to take care of it.

"You should really brush your hair more often."

It made me jump when I heard Nerissa talk.

Nerissa gripped my hair tighter as she worked through yet another knot.

I pressed my fingers onto the back of my head as I yelped, "Ow!"

The water below me stirred at the movement of my shoe against the water. I waited until the water was still again. The water reflected my face and I took the time to study it. My eyebrows furrowed as I noticed how chapped my lips were, translucent skin peeling from the dip on my bottom lip. I looked down at my nails. Dirt encrusted the inner lining of my nails. Most of them were long because of the inability to cut them, but some of the nails had broken off and left an unsatisfying rigid top. I patted my cheek, looking back down at my reflection. My skin looked patchy even through the hazy appearance of the water. There were sections of darker pigment surrounding my eyes and the sides of my nose. Were my lips always this colorless? My eyes trailed down towards the rest of my body. I was skinner than usual even though there was no need to eat during the Challenge. I looked away, buttoning up the shirt Kace gave me.

"You have so much to say, Nerissa," I said as I pressed my lips together.

Nerissa paused as I turned slightly to her so I could see the left side of her face. "Hmm?"

"You stay silent until spoken to, why's that? In arguments you have so much to put forward; you obviously think a lot. Why don't you speak?"

Nerissa hung her head a bit lower as she continued to pause before speaking. "The louder you are, the fewer people will want to continue listening to you. But when you only bring up what's important, people will listen. People think silent people are smart, but in reality they just appreciate when they don't have to listen."

I huffed, "So, Spencer makes people listen to him."

Nerissa smiled a bit. "Spencer, Spencer, he has a personality. I'll give him that."

I furrowed my eyebrows. "But he's related to you."

Nerissa stopped and yanked the brush from my hair. I reached for my roots in pain. "Who told you that?"

I let an anxious breath out. "You two just—look the same."

Nerissa nodded slowly before speaking. "Spencer understands emotions, but he isn't empathic towards them."

I winced as Nerissa moved the hairbrush near me. "Are you calling him manipulative?"

"Mhm, something like that."

No denying it, huh?

"What's that supposed to mean?"

"Spencer knows somethings that he shouldn't be keeping a secret, but I'm going to let him reveal it by his own means." Nerissa paused again. "Either way, Spencer might be my blood, but I believe in you." She looked up at the boulders in front of us and the cloud of fog surrounding the body-shaped figure above the rocks. "Marissa was like you. Strong-willed. We need more people like Marissa. More people like you."

"Mia!" I was transported back to where I had been before.

I shivered as I looked up. Kace furrowed his eyebrows in a slightly worried fashion.

"Sorry," I whispered, "I was just wondering if you have information on Courtney. Maybe like a file or something. She's obviously modified, but I was curious if she was aware of her modifications?"

Kace used his palm to hoist himself up. He nodded, "Yeah, I'm not sure about the details on her or anything, but you could ask Lauren since you and Queens get along so well." Kace shrugged his shoulders as he moved towards his desk to rearrange the loose papers on it.

"Huh, yeah, I was just wondering how she knew Spencer's nickname that I have for him."

Kace gave a half-smile; the blood that made his cheeks pink drained from his face. "Excuse me?"

I sucked at my teeth. "You heard what I said."

Kace let out a nervous laugh. "I mean, I have no information on that. You must have misheard her." I continued to listen to Kace's argument as I shifted towards the desk table. I peered down. Intertwined black cords were connected to a series of outlets under the desk. Kace was keeping his hands busy and placed his coding book on the edge of the table. *Perfect.* "I mean, evidently, Courtney is human so if she heard said nickname then she's obviously going to use it. But I don't understand how this correlates with whether or not she is aware of her modifications. Which also leads to the point that she's human and some things aren't in control of the Techs."

I nodded, but in reality I had no idea what he was saying. I had one thing on my mind: the cords under his desk. If I pulled those cords, anything related to modifications would have to disappear. Courtney wouldn't be coded, our High Tide abilities wouldn't exist, and the monsters and beasts created by Kace as well as any appearance changes made by Lauren would disappear. I couldn't protect myself with my Neutral abilities anymore. I huffed.

"Mia," Kace said. He sounded afraid. "Mia," he said more urgently. "What are—" he exclaimed as I ducked down and yanked at the cords. Kace's hands pressed down on my thigh to try and push me away. I hastily reached for the dagger that rested on the pocket in the center of my shield. I aimed it towards him. "Jesus!" he yelped as he clutched his chest. I swung the dagger away from him and towards the cords. To my surprise, the dagger wasn't sharp enough to cut the cords with one slice. I pressed the dagger in the bunch back and forth until visible tears let copper cords protrude out.

I exhaled slowly as I stood up. Kace was still applying pressure on the cut near his ribs.

I placed my palms on the desk. "You got a USB with coding information or something, Kace?"

He groaned, "Up there." He motioned to a USB sticking out of a monitor screen. I reached on my tiptoes to grab it. I swiped the coding book from the table.

"Thanks, Kace," I nodded in approval to him. "You're a terrible liar by the way."

Kace stared at me for a few seconds as I scrunched up my face in concentration. "Mia," he remarked, "You can't teleport."

"Yep, the consequences of my own actions." I pressed my lips together as I pushed the book more comfortably in my arms. The corners of Kace's lips lifted up as he turned his head away from me to suppress his laughter. I smiled slightly at him as I struggled to open the door with my forefinger.

I gasped as I saw the rest of the Tech building. The building used to have a lavish interior design with carefully curated walls and chandeliers, but the building now was made of drywall. The drywall was chipping, some areas had gashes that allowed the wood underneath to peak out. The floor was slabs of partially sanded wood. I pressed my shoe against a strip of wood that stuck up.

I walked on the floor as softly as I could, trying not to alarm Lauren by the new changes. The floor creaked underneath me. I held my breath as I walked through an opening between two sections of drywall.

I stepped outside. There was no grass. It wasn't very surprising that the grass wasn't real, noting that there was no access to sunlight and grass usually didn't come in multiple colors. What was shocking, however, was the pillars surrounding the body of salty water still remained. Someone actually built those pillars. Nerissa, as usual, was seated on the bridge, facing away from Marissa and her boulders.

I frowned. The bubble still didn't make sense. There was nothing scientific about a layer of fog hoisting a forty pound child.

A presumably dead child.

The cord I pulled gave back some realism in my life. None of the fictional things I'd been seeing for the past year were real. Everything came from the imagination of Kace and past Techs. It irked me that one piece didn't fit in. Was there a cord I didn't pull? Did Lauren have an extra computer hidden in the room she was always in? Was Kace still lying to me when he told me I had unplugged everything?

No. Kace never said I pulled all the cords. He only cooperated with what I said. I pressed my lips together as I motioned to Nerissa.

I heaved as I gestured the book towards Nerissa. I flinched. Her hair no longer was dyed red and was its natural black color. Her nose was wider, but everything else looked the same.

I huffed, "Can you take this? It's important."

Nerissa held eye contact with me as she let the book drop from my grip and onto her arms. She exhaled. "Do you like liars, Mia?"

My face twitched. "What do you mean?"

"Spencer, Kace, Maybelle. They're all liars. Do you like liars? Do you enjoy their company?"

I looked down. "Are you a liar?"

"Define a lie."

Chapter Thirty

Spare a Heart

I placed the gauze on the desk near the chair Kace was now sitting in. He reached for the gauze as he brought up the edge of his shirt to his teeth so he could hold it up. He carefully wrapped the gauze around his torso as I peeled the tape and ripped it. Kace lifted the end of the gauze so I could press the tape on it.

I sat on the desk, next to the chair he was sitting in. "I'm sorry; it was kind of an in-the-moment type situation."

"It's fine." Kace sucked at the inside of his cheek before continuing. "I'm more worried about Lauren than the cut anyway."

I laughed nervously. "She's going to be livid."

Kace looked down. "It doesn't matter right now. Let's ignore what happened." He paused before smiling. "Tell me your plan. How are you going to make sure Spencer doesn't escape?"

"Uh-well, I was planning on talking to him." I furrowed my eyebrows. I hadn't actually thought about how I was planning on convincing Spencer, I was just planning on doing so.

Kace laughed at me. "Talking works. But, barely knowing Spencer, I don't think he takes other opinions very well. The both of you are very strong-willed."

"Yeah, I get that a lot."

He looked up at me, smiling slightly. "I don't doubt it." He seemed to study my face before continuing. "But, here's the thing, Mia. I think you should let the future do its thing. If he leaves, that's his fault. Obviously, I won't stop you from trying to convince him, but I'm just saying that you should spare your heart."

"Spare my heart? I'm not *infatuated* with him or anything."

Kace raised his eyebrows. "Okay. If you say so." He grinned at me, but slowly his smile started to fade. "Mia, I'm sorry about Courtney. It's part of my job to code information in her and I wasn't expecting for you two to meet."

"It's fine, Kace." I pressed my lips together. I reached into my pocket and pulled out another gauze roll. "For later," I said as I placed it in his palm.

He looked at me as he placed it on the desk and stood up. "You know, he might convince you to leave too," Kace complained.

"I'm not leaving. I didn't partner with Maybelle to not get what I wanted."

The left corner of Kace's face twitched up slightly, but he wasn't completely smiling. "That's good. I don't want you to leave. I think we're starting to become friends."

I could feel my cheeks getting hot. "Even though I scratched you?"

Kace looked down and picked at the gauze beside him as he stood up. "A little more than a scratch." He looked up and grinned at me. Kace was an unusually optimistic person, never once bashing the lack of logic of my plans, unlike Spencer. Kace was always light-hearted with his sentences and always smiling. But this was the first time I could completely tell that his smile was genuine. I wanted to see him actually smile more often. He stepped closer to me, rolling a strand of my hair in between his fingers. "I suppose there's no chance of getting the book and USB back?"

"No. I'm not giving it back to you."

Kace's smile faded a bit. "You have no idea what you did, do you?" He pointed to the cord. "High Tide's monsters disappear with that, sure. But without *my* Tech work, you're not protected against hunger or cuts." He looked down at his scratch and then back up at me. He paused and relaxed his tensed-up eyebrows. "What are you going to do with them anyway?" he spoke more softly.

I looked down. "I don't know."

"See, you don't even know," he scoffed. Kace huffed then opened his mouth to speak. "I'm sorry. I'm just worried about what Lauren would think."

I nodded as he moved his hand to my cheek. There was a small thump sound that caused Kace to twitch. He immediately dropped his hand and looked away.

He took a step back and mumbled, "You should go."

Chapter Thirty-one

Siblings

There was a fifty-fifty chance Courtney would do what I wanted her to do. She'd either keep Spencer from escaping, or help him escape. With a lack of modifications on High Tide, I had no idea what her new personality would be.

My breath hitched because of something heavy pushing down on my chest. Courtney's arms were cold and skinny. The light hairs on her arms stood up and the bones near her elbows protruded out. She was fragile-looking, but she definitely was strong. "Mia!"

I gave her a half-smile. "Courtney."

Courtney finally let go of her grip on me and rested her hands on my shoulders as she grinned at me once more. I wiggled away from her to sit on her bed.

I looked her in the eye after she turned towards me. "Do you know of a man named Elliot?"

Courtney shrugged her shoulders. "Sure! He was your relative, right? Talking about relatives, do you have any siblings?"

She's trying to change the subject. I went along with it. "No. Only child."

"Oh! I have a brother," she shrugged. "I loved him so much."

That's definitely not true. "You said you hated him before."

Courtney sat down next to me. "Love, hate. Same difference."

"Courtney. Did you or did you not meet Elliot?"

She huffed, her smile disappearing slightly. "Yes. I've met him."

That happened around thirty years ago. If the modifications were truly gone, she'd be at least forty years old, yet she didn't look a day over sixteen.

"How old are you?"

"Mia," she smiled in aspiration, "I'm not stupid; I know what you're getting at. I'm not modified. I'm just *me.*"

"Did he starve because of the aftermath of the challenge or did you kill him?"

Courtney gasped, her mouth hanging open and her eyebrows pressed together. "How could you ask me that? You know, I was starting to think we were becoming friends."

I frowned. *That's what Kace told me.* My jaw clenched as I stood up and pointed at Courtney. "What the hell are you? Are you trying to get a reaction out of me?"

Courtney looked at me plainly, slightly confused. "Well, if I was, wouldn't it be working?"

I huffed as I glared at her. I stood up and walked towards the door. The door was all metal like the rest of the room with a matching metal bar that if you pushed the door would open. Not for Courtney though. The bar scanned people's fingertips and wouldn't budge if it recognized Courtney's hand.

"What did you come here for?" Courtney sounded upset. "To interrogate me?"

"I came to open your door, as you asked before," I said as I slammed her door shut.

Chapter Thirty-two

All My Fault

"The last time you had a personal discussion with me you were telling me how you thought I shouldn't worry and should escape from the Trap." Spencer pressed his eyebrows together and stuck out his bottom lip in mock sincerity.

"Spencer—"

He laughed. "No. No. And now you're going to tell me that I shouldn't escape. The irony. All because of some words on your arm. Now, I know you're going to want to speak, but I'm not going to let you. That prophecy or whatever was made by the Queens and I don't trust them. So I'm taking my chances."

My bottom lip hung down in confusion. "So, that's it? You're not even going to listen to my side of the argument?"

"No, I'm not. Look, you're just worried that I'm not going to be with you anymore, but you have a choice to escape with Courtney and me."

My lips tensed. "Hold up. You *and* Courtney? Since when was Courtney involved in this? You've only met her like two times and now you're planning on risking your life with her?"

"Mia."

"No. Do you know what she is? Are you not skeptical?"

Spencer shook his hand. He pointed to his nails where fire would appear if I didn't have that interaction with Kace in the Tech room. "It doesn't work anymore which means that she isn't modified anymore. She's safe."

"She's not, Spence. I just talked to her. It's almost as if the modifications got to her brain. She's exactly the same."

"She has the same personality because she's human. Humans have consistent personalities, Mia."

"I don't care. Just go."

"So, you're letting me escape with Courtney." Spencer looked at me skeptically and stared at him back. He realized he wasn't going to get a response from me and nodded. "I'm going to win for the both of us. Okay, Mia?" Spencer placed his hand on my shoulder and I shrugged it away.

"I don't care about winning."

And that was true. There was no point in winning vicariously. Not after all my efforts to pull myself together. I managed to befriend all the Queens and convinced them to help me. If I wanted, I could be Queen myself.

And with Kace's modifications, I used to be the most powerful person in High Tide. I was a Neutral and alongside Kace, I could do anything.

I wasn't here for my mother anymore; I was here for myself. And that is the best way of winning.

Chapter Thirty-three

Morality

There was something beautiful about Kace. That means there's something beautiful about his monsters too. Kace was perfectly kind inside and out and, although he designed evil, his monsters were ingrained with kindness too. I recalled the monster I saw Spencer fight. The monster had almost caressed him once it admitted defeat.

Courtney was a different breed of monster. She wasn't willing to only block Spencer from escaping, she wanted him dead.

Even if that meant she had to trust the prophecy and help him escape from the place she was coded to keep him contained. But I doubted that she was only coded to keep her guests within High Tide. She was created to kill them off. And soon that code of killing became a habit which became instinct.

But inside, Courtney was human. The Techs changed her. I wondered if the other monsters were once human too.

But Kace didn't make Courtney. Kace was given Courtney, and told to make her worse. And he listened.

I couldn't tell who fell deeper into the Trap of peer pressure. Kace or Courtney. A girl passed from generation to generation, who went from being coded as mean to evil being a part of her, even when unplugged. And a boy whose only personality was derived from toxic positivity and the protection of Lauren.

Peer pressure sucks the morality from us. But then again, who am I to judge? Because if I am only powerful with Kace's modifications, I am just as bad as him.

Chapter Thirty-four

To be a God

Maybelle calls me her mediator. There's no need for me anyway. Both Nerissa and Maybelle have loud personalities when need be; they wouldn't listen to me anyway. Maybelle, however, was never mad at me, but never ceased to not find an opportunity to yell at Nerissa. I couldn't tell if it was because of Maybelle's past prejudices against anything pertaining to Marissa, the fact that I was a child in her eyes, or if she was manipulating me into liking her more.

Maybelle thrived on instilling fear. It made her feel superior, above all others. She wanted not only the power or the immortality of being a Queen, she wanted both. She wanted to be a god. *Gods don't manipulate.*

Manipulation. That was more of Spencer's thing. He called it *analysis and debate.* But why would a manipulator tell others he was manipulating them, anyway?

Maybelle smiled one of those smiles people do when they're angry. Her teeth were clenched, but her upper lip was raised. "What the *hell* is this?" She clicked her tongue. She was wearing a black tank top with sewn lace on the straps and the hemming on the bottom of the shirt. Covering the rest of her exposed skin were browning vines. Vines have thorns on them and with High Tide's modifications, no one could bleed. Unless the computers weren't working.

Maybelle had gashes down from her shoulders to her ribs. Covered in thick, dried red.

I gagged. The room smelled of copper.

Gods don't bleed.

"You told her to enter the Tech building by herself and, as a curious teen, she would likely go back and see what else the building had to offer," Nerissa justified nonchalantly. I valued how calm she was during this situation.

"Are you saying *this* is my fault?" Maybelle brashly gestured towards the red on her body.

"This isn't my fault either. I was not involved at all in this situation."

"No, you're right. It isn't your fault." Maybelle Monel continued after she stuck her nail between my two eyes. "It's hers." I squeezed my eyes shut; it hurt my eyes to focus on her finger that was too close to my face.

I dropped the shield I had in my hand. In the middle of the shield lay my dagger in the metal case that was formed to hold weapons with a dagger-like handle. The *clanging* sound of the shield dropping rang in my ears. I tilted my head towards Maybelle.

What would Spencer do in this situation? "I'm just a child."

Maybelle turned to Nerissa. "Didn't Spencer make the exact same statement?" Maybelle laughed. "Are you trying to be like him, Mia?"

I frowned. "Of course not; I'm just telling you that I shouldn't have that much pressure upheld on me since I'm less mature than the rest of you."

Maybelle smiled one of her trademark grins where her nose wrinkles up. Maybelle took a second to chuckle. "You *love* Spencer so much, right? So much that you'd lie to *me* to keep him safe? But, you don't even know his truth."

What truth? Was she saying that Spencer was keeping a *truth* from me?

I couldn't deny that I thought about that possibility before. He has been seeming secretive for a while now.

Gods don't manipulate. Gods tell the truth. Was Maybelle telling the truth?

Maybelle looked down to smile. She was no longer smiling at me, but at herself. She continued, "He knows. He knows the killer. He knows who murdered your mom. His loving mother was the one to bail said killer. Mia. Do you know whom I'm talking about?

I rasped out, "No!"

Maybelle laughed by using a huff from her nose. "You don't have to tell me, but don't deny it. You know who *she* is."

I wobbled from my position. I furrowed my eyebrows as I hugged myself. The bridge was wood. The bridge was flammable.

The bridge was on fire. There was a whimper from Maybelle as she inched away from the tube made of white and yellow paper. It reeked of tobacco.

Gods don't fear.

The slender hands carried a cigarette pack and a lighter. The lighter was hard to miss: it was rectangular shaped with an image of Hestia on it. Her dark eyes gleamed. She placed her finger between her top and bottom canines and slightly bit down as she smiled widely. Allison removed her finger to bite down on her lower lip, still maintaining her grin. The Royalty had the pleasure of having access to clothing changing and Allison's fashion sense was never suppressed. Today she wore a black Gothic dress with white detailing at the collar and edges of her sleeves. To pair with the fluffy laced dress, she wore striped socks that reached her knees. Her large mass of hair was styled into box braids which helped keep the strands away from her face. She looked youthful.

Maybelle wept in pain as a spark of flame flew towards her. *Fire.*

"Maybelle!" Allison exclaimed as she reached in for a one-sided hug. She pointed the white cigarette box to Maybelle. "Care for one?"

Maybelle's smile had disappeared. She glared at me. "No. I do not want a cigarette."

Allison looked at me, and bended over to my height. "What about you, love?"

Maybelle scoffed "That's a child."

Allison smiled even wider, the edges of her pink gums showing. *"She's* a child. *She*—Now, Mia, do you want one?"

"You're exactly whom I'm looking for," Nerissa chimed in, gesturing to Maybelle. She seemed indifferent to Allison's presence, not seeming too excited to have extra company. Maybelle frowned at her as she zipped a sweater over herself. Nerissa turned towards the rocks. Nerissa continued, "Cords were pulled. The Tech building is completely empty. And, yet, I don't know how Marissa is still up there."

Nerissa pointed to the gas bubble to where Marissa supposedly was.

Allison bit the corner of her bottom lip. "There has to be some sort of computer that the kid hasn't unplugged yet. Mia, you've seen an extra room you haven't been in the Tech building yet, right?"

"Yes. There's a room that Lauren stays locked up in," I responded.

"Hold up." Maybelle sounded irked. *"Mia* unplugged everything?" She turned towards me. "Do you have *any* idea what you're doing?"

Allison laughed at her. "Who else? The Tech boy himself? She's the only chick with courage." She cupped her palm around my head and used it to mess up my hair, lovingly.

There was a bold aura to Allison and her kind words to me made me feel validated in a way no one close to me could ever make me feel.

Maybelle didn't like the compliment, as presumed. She was jealous and I could not blame her. I barely knew Allison, but here I was, feeding off her praise.

Allison nodded her head to acknowledge the silence before starting again. "What's done is done. You're human now. You bleed! You can still stay here and not worry about getting arrested on Earth."

Maybelle pursed her lips. "What are you saying?"

Nerissa looked down to remark. "She's saying she's getting rid of your position as a Queen."

Maybelle turned her head away from all of us.

Allison ignored the newfound heavy feelings in the room as she pressed the flame to her lighter onto the white of the cigarette. "See, Mia, before all this I didn't even need this thing!" She smiled and jabbed my arm with her shoulder to make sure I knew she was only messing with me. "Anyway, *May,* I'd put your guard up, because I got a new competitor. And they're taking your place.

Gods don't have competitors.

She was no god.

No matter how much she wanted to be one.

Chapter Thirty-five

Analysis and Debate: Explained

Spencer says that everyone falls into a specific personality type. Although he valued having his own wits and relying on information he came up with himself, he was obsessed with understanding others. The MBTI personality types made sense to him. He became infatuated with withholding so much information on others after receiving their four letters.

I'm an INTP. Or at least that's what the online test and Spencer told me I was. Introverted. Intuitive. Thinking. Perceiving. Apparently, it means I value truth.

It's not wrong.

Spencer wouldn't tell me his personality type. Not surprising, since he keeps his feelings on the low, but it kind of hurts, coming from your best friend.

But that's only Spencer's analysis. His debate is where he uses his opposing candidate's weakness to provide a sucker punch argument. That unfortunately works, the majority of the time.

He gets what he wants when he wants it. After a little bit of arguing, of course.

He doesn't have emotions. Only the emotions you want

him to have. He understands people. Not to show sympathy, but for manipulation. Every piece of information he collects is used against you. Everything you say or do can be used against you in a court of law.

Innocent until proven guilty. We all love to throw that phrase around. But it doesn't matter if you are or are not guilty. What matters is if you're viewed as guilty. Innocent until *seen.* Spencer does the seeing and in return, he's always innocent.

He might see me as four letters that once appeared on my phone screen, but I see him like a scorpion. A hard shell that protects him from others. The stinger protects him too, a more destructive protection method. We hope that if we ignore the scorpion, it'll leave us alone too. We are afraid of the inflicted pain from its sting, but the scorpion is scared of the humans hovering over it.

I think we often ignore the shell. But more importantly, we don't even see its fleshy inside.

I'm not scared of Spencer. He's only a boy who hopes to live up to his father's expectations. He's scared of letting the man, who risked his life flying across a border to give his future child a chance, he's afraid of letting the poor man down. Spencer is afraid of failure.

I wondered if he'd be scared of me if I told him that I know him more than he thinks. I also wondered if he knew what empathy was.

A teacher once told him he overthinks like a female. He was crying that day over his grades. I yelled at our teacher for being misogynistic. I got detention and that night I overheard Spencer's mom yelling at him for making his father cry because of his grades. It made me want to cry.

The detention was worth it.

Chapter Thirty-six

To Be A God: Explained

I could be a Queen right now if I wanted to. Maybelle was now mortal because of the lack of Tech work in High Tide and the majority of her body was already underwater. Her body was already fragile; the thorns that covered her body imprinted on her causing her to bleed. She finally got the covering of thorns off her body, but she still had crusted blood remaining on her body. Maybelle's arms were rested on the edge of the pier. The seawater covered her body from the shoulders down. She wasn't looking at me; she was picking at a scab on her shoulder, watching as fresh blood trickled down her finger and arm.

It would be easy to have her drown. I could take my shoe and kick her head down. One shove and she'd be underwater forever. If she died, someone would have to take her place.

But we had a deal. If I helped her to make sure that the High Tide Competitors didn't take her place, she'd bring my mom back.

I wasn't like the other Queens. They were all greedy. Greedy for power or greedy for a luxurious magical life that Earth didn't have to offer.

We all have a public image. We are all Queens, it's our

formal side. The face we put on for others. Maybelle is a Queen who wants power and to be immortal, but that's not who she is on the inside.

Maybelle and I have people who think they're friends with us, but we aren't friends with them ourselves.

But there's one difference: Maybelle doesn't have loyalty. There's no loyalty in her heart like what I have for Spencer. I owe him.

Maybelle runs on making deals. You help her and eventually, she'll help you back. That way she has no responsibility to take care of you.

Internally, Maybelle and I are lonely.

Maybelle tapped a beat on the wood of the pier with her fingers. She leaned forward her under-bust resting against the pier so that I could hear her better. "You need Lauren on your side, Mia. She has access to the Tech things you need to bring back your mom. So, let's be honest. What exactly did you do in that Tech room?"

I paused, thinking about how I could phrase what happened properly. "I attacked the Technician and used that as a distraction to pull the cords."

Maybelle nodded. "Did you take anything?"

"No," I lied.

Maybelle rubbed her arm as she spoke. "Good." Maybelle reached her hand towards me for me to pull. I hoisted her rub and she wrung the water out from her hair. She looked down at me as she pulled a plaid, pink dress over her and tied the strings of the dress to her waist. "You're on my side, right, Mia?" She leaned forward to clutch my shoulder as she pointed to a brown house in the near distance from us. "See that right there? That's my house. With the lack of modifications, you'll feel tired soon."

She removed her hand from me to reach into a black, snake-skin bag beside my feet. She pulled out a gold watch.

There were flowers built onto the gold chained strap of it. I looked down at the flowers embellished on the shield on my shoulder. They matched the watch. Maybelle guided my hand into hers. She pulled up the nylon sleeves of the green jacket Kace gave me. She delicately placed the watch on my wrist and flipped it over to clip it together. My hand twitched from the cold feeling of the untouched chain.

I looked down at the time. 6:11. I looked back up at Maybelle as she opened her mouth again to speak. "I'll meet you there at ten."

Chapter Thirty-seven

Sunlight

I stared down at the blackened wood in front of me. I had a feeling the wood used to be structured as a house. The wood was old and soft-looking as if some sort of water had softened it. A few scattered shelf mushrooms were growing on the wood. The air smelled of petrichor and trees.

Trees.

I looked to my left. In the distance were trees. A whole forest. I reached into my pocket. The letter Lauren gave me when I was searching through that same forest was in my pocket.

Even I didn't need Spencer to realize that trees need sunlight to grow. I looked above us and saw a layer of rough stone and dirt. We were under all the people who dwelled on Earth. I recalled when modifications allowed for clouds to float above us, but now it was the natural stone covering that was clearly visible. Even with modifications, there was never a sun. Trees grew because of the way Tech's modified them. And, even without modifications there still wasn't a sun.

I looked around. I leaned away from the houses to take a good look at what was around us. With no sun and no modifications, there had to be some sort of light source that allowed us to see down here. I looked at the house in front of me. Even the houses didn't have the lights on them like the ones on Earth did.

I pursed my lips. With Marissa still being supernaturally suspended in air, the irregular growth of trees, and an irregular sense of light source, there still had to be some sort of modification that still existed on High Tide.

I furrowed my eyebrows. I thought I'd pulled all the cords in the Tech room.

But, like I told Allison, Lauren had a secret room. There was no doubt in my mind that there was another computer there.

I sighed as I looked at the watch Maybelle gave me. It was around six o'clock when I last checked, but after having a conversation with Maybelle and then Nerissa time went by. Walking from the bridge to the house in front of me took about thirty minutes. So at that time, it was around seven. I noted where the minute hand was on the clock. *9:11.* I huffed. I guess I took a while to investigate the wood next to the house and evaluate whether I believed there was still a running computer here. Maybelle said she'd be here at ten. I had time.

The house in front of me was on the smaller side, looking more like a cottage rather than a house. There was seemingly only one level to the house because the windows were all in one row. There were four light brown pillars, two on each side, that led to the door that was a darker shade of brown than the rest of the house. The house itself was made of multi-colored brown bricks. The yard wasn't much of a yard. There were no plants and no grass, but concrete. I walked towards the house. There was a dark brown, standing garden bed. It was filled with dirt to the top. Small, damp planks of wood were stacked on top. Small mushrooms peeked out from the top. I looked up. The window in front of me was long, but not wide. There were two panels to the window; the one on top was the shorter one and the other one was long. I couldn't see through the window due to a brown covering over it, from the inside. I brushed my left hand across the side of the window and onto the bricks. The bricks were gritty and rough. My hand then touched something smooth. It was a sign. Normally, on Earth, these signs had numbers on them to inform others of the address of the house, but this sign had Maybelle's name. I wondered if all the houses had everyone's name on them.

I turned to the house in front of Maybelle's. Similarly, the yard was concrete. This house was a gray bungalow with a low sloping roof. The steps to the house looked unstable, yet I placed my right foot on the lowest stair anyway. The plank creaked but didn't move. I shrugged my shoulders and walked up four more steps to the house. I pressed my eyebrows together when I saw the door. Next to the door was a sign that had Lauren's name. I huffed as I turned towards the door again. The door was bolted shut with planks of wood nailed to the doorway. I reached down to my shield to grab my dagger. I slid the dagger flat down the non-visible side of the first plank. Once I got a good grip on the handle and sharp edge of my dagger, I pulled at it, hoping that the plank would push off. I frantically gasped and dropped my dagger as the sharp part of it dug into my skin. My hand shook as I realized that the cut wouldn't heal itself. I reminded myself to breathe as I rubbed the flowing blood on my pants. My clothes were covered with dirt and random filth already; the bloodstain wasn't even the most noticeable stain on it.

Being self-aware of my clothing and the filth on it, I had a sudden urge to take a shower. I sighed in relief, realizing that Maybelle's house probably had running water.

I walked down the steps, away from Lauren's house. I turned back towards her house. The windows weren't bolted shut.

9:27.
Is time going extremely fast or something?
I couldn't risk it.
Plus, I was curious about the other Queen's houses.

The house neighboring Maybelle's was a rich purple color. The house had two levels, but the top one only had one window. The yard was curiously not concrete but multicolored stones. The two doors to the house were clear. I peered through them. The interior design was too dark to properly see what was inside the house. I pulled at the door's handle. *Locked.* I pressed my lips together. I stepped down to see the sign on the house. I laughed slightly. I should have realized right away that the house was Allison's. Allison was the only Queen with a unique taste while the rest of the queens preferred to be more subtle with their style.

I walked towards Maybelle's house with a determination to take a shower.

I paused at the doorway. Maybelle's house only had one room. Well, technically two. A wall with a curved opening and no door separated the two areas of the house. I stepped inside. On the side of the house I was in, there was a brown circular table, a fireplace, and a few kitchen appliances. There was a black gas stove with an oven underneath, a shiny sink, and a microwave. I turned my head, looking for a fridge until my hand came in contact with a mini-fridge. I opened the door and noticed three, small bottles of water.

I could suddenly feel the dryness in my throat. I reached for the bottle to my right. The water felt cool to touch. The cap was thin and securely screwed onto the bottle. It took some strength to twist it off. I listened to the cracking and crinkling sound of the bottle as I drained the water inside it. I reached for the second bottle, my throat still not satiated. I threw the bottles in the can right next to the counter with the microwave.

There was a cream-colored, damask wallpaper that covered the area of the house I was standing in. I exhaled. I remembered that type of wallpaper from my mom's house. My house.

Before I moved. Before the house was set on fire.

I squeezed my eyes shut and focused on the scent of the house. The house smelled of old wood and a faint whiff of gasoline.

My body felt weak, almost as if I was straining my muscles to merely stand up *Exhaustion*. I haven't felt the feeling of wanting to collapse in a while. I pulled a wooden chair towards me as I drained the last bottle of water from the fridge.

I stood up. I still wanted to change and take a shower.

As a replacement for a door, Maybelle put a beaded curtain to decorate the opening in the wall. I pushed the strings of clear gems away as I walked through it. I was relieved to notice a small room with a lock. A bathroom. I opened the door and there I saw a shower. I sighed. I looked at the mirror. My jacket was completely soiled and the black shirt under was stuck to my skin by sweat. I cringed. I stepped away from the bathroom to examine a closet that laid to my left. It was a dark brown that sort of matched the brown of the kitchen table. I pulled the two doors open. There was a top compartment that had plush, brown towels. The clothes in the closet were all suited for Maybelle's style with white tiered skirts, fur-lined jackets, light pink button-downs, and latex go-go boots. I reached for a towel and set it down on the dressing table next to the closet. I peeled the clothing from my body and deposited it in the trash. Except for the jacket. Throwing away all the clothes Kace had given me felt wrong, no matter how dirty the clothes were. I rinsed the jacket in the sink. The jacket was made of a slippery, plastic material so the grime on it slipped right off. The outside of the jacket was relatively dry, but the soft inner fabric of it was soaking wet. I wrung the jacket before hanging it on the dressing table's mirror.

I walked back to the bathroom and turned on the shower's faucet. I normally preferred warmer showers, but today I had the sudden urge to use cold water. I hunched over in the shower. The coolness of the water pressed against my sore muscles. I had no energy to rub the sweat off me. I was tired. I haven't felt this way in forever.

I almost felt guilty for pulling those plugs in the Tech Room. I had no justifiable answer for doing so besides the hope that Courtney would go back to normal and that Kace would stop lying to me. Neither situation came true. I sighed as I wrapped the textured towel around me.

I was comforted by realizing that the lack of modifications wasn't too terrible since High Tide's monsters no longer existed. I doubted if I could trust Kace to continue to steer his monsters away from me like he was doing before. Now he had no option to do such things, which was a relief.

No Tech access, no new monsters.

The cotton pants I tried putting on kept sticking to the remaining water on my legs. I forgot how hard it was to wear clothes after coming out from a shower. I slipped on a pair of blue, plaid pajama pants and a plain, baggy black shirt. It took me forever to find suitable clothing. It was almost as if Maybelle slept in her fancy clothes.

I placed the watch Maybelle gave me on my wrist again. *10:04.* She was supposed to be here four minutes ago.

I shrugged and decided to wait for her. I sat down at the kitchen table again. I reached for the empty water bottle I left on the table. Next to the bottle was a brown ceramic, bowl-like incense holder. I reached for that instead, letting go of the bottle. I smiled. I could burn some incense to make it smell better in here. I grasped onto the handle of the kitchen drawer. A few sticks of incense were wrapped in plastic. I pulled out one and placed the stick close to the heated stove. Smoke immediately released from it and I placed it on the incense holder.

The incense no longer had any scent; it must have been old. There was no point in burning it. Although I never was keen on things that burned or related to fire, the smoke from the incense was mesmerizing. To be afraid of fire was kind of childish. Incense was flammable, but eventually, it would extinguish itself. To be afraid of limited experiences didn't make sense.

I let the incense continue burning as I decided to finally go to sleep even though Maybelle still wasn't here yet. I looked at the room. There was a maroon couch and one loft bed. The loft was even completely a loft. It was a flat piece of wood attached to the wall with a mattress on it. There was no actual ladder connected to the loft, but Maybelle had placed a construction ladder to give access to it. The couch was a maroon color that felt like cotton. There were no pillows on the couch, but there was a pink and green quilt folded neatly on the backrest of it.

I heard the door creak open. *Maybelle.*

She groaned slightly. I walked over to her to see what was up. She picked up the incense holder and plucked the stick out. "This is flammable," she remarked.

"I know. It's incense," I stated as she stuck the burning incense in a stream of cold water coming from the sink.

"You have to be careful." Maybelle deposited the incense in the garbage can near her. She brushed my shoulder as she walked past me to look in her closet. She pulled out a black, silk nightdress and a towel. She slung her items over her shoulder as she pointed to the loft. "Go to bed."

"I can sleep on the couch," I offered.

"No," Maybelle declined as she shut the bathroom door behind her.

Chapter Thirty-eight

Shelf

The pants in my hands felt like a wool material. They were soft, but not for athletics. Maybelle told me I should wear something decent since I no longer needed to fight any monsters. She had also given me a cream-colored knit top, but the material felt itchy so I kept on the black shirt I was wearing last night. I zipped up the fly on the pants. The pants weren't meant to be too loose, but since they were in Maybelle's size, and I was shorter than her, they bunched up at the ends. They were also loose around the mid-area. The looseness made the pants more comfortable.

I squinted my eyes, trying to remember the dream I just had. My reminiscing was cut short as my stomach rumbled.

I was hungry yesterday, but it wasn't to the extent I was feeling now. My stomach burned from the lack of food I'd had. I turned towards my left shoulder to look out the window. Maybelle was outside tending to her empty garden bed. I rapped at the window. Maybelle looked up at me, confused. I pressed my eyebrows together and shook my head as I raised my palms in similar confusion. Maybelle gestured for me to come to her. I swung my hair away from me as I pushed the door open. Maybelle was plucking the white mushrooms from the wood on her garden bed. She pushed a handful of them on my palms.

"They're edible. Shelf mushrooms," Maybelle said as she inspected one.

"Right," I gestured my pointer finger towards her. "You used to be able to move plants or whatever."

She scoffed, "With that logic, you must be all-knowing since you used to have every ability! You used to be a Neutral or whatever." She sneered as she sauntered towards the door.

I grasped the edge of the door before Maybelle's force shut it. "You're a meanie."

"How mature. I thought you were thirteen now?" she laughed good-heartedly this time. She thrust a skillet towards me. I ducked, the pan barely skimming my head. I reached for the handle on the pan and placed it on the stove. The handle was still cold, even after Maybelle's tight grip on it.

Maybelle had already washed the mushrooms and now was covering them in olive oil. She opened her pantry door and grabbed a mason jar with dried rosemary. She pulled the leaves off the stalk with ease and then reached for her pink salt shaker. Pink Himalayan salt came from the opening and dusted the mushrooms. She turned towards me and coated my pan in olive oil. I turned the skillet in a circular motion in response. She raised her eyebrows at me. "You okay with spice?" she asked as she reached behind my back to get red pepper flakes. I nodded as she poured the red flakes into the bowl without bothering to see what my response was. She gave the mushrooms a quick toss and dumped the ingredients onto my pan. The mushrooms gave a satisfying sizzle. Maybelle huffed as she was exhausted and collapsed on one of her kitchen chairs.

It was stupid of me to have barely cooked before, but I have never sautéed food on a stove. My mom didn't trust a five-year-old to help her cook (thank God) and Elaine didn't want my dirt-soiled fingers messing around with her pristine stove either. I took the thongs beside me to hold up a cut-up strip of mushroom towards Maybelle. The mushroom was soggy and completely covered in oil. I twitched as a drop of the golden oil dropped onto the floor.

I gave Maybelle a questioning look. "Is it supposed to look like this?"

Maybelle didn't look up. "Yeah. More or less."

I raised my eyebrows in denial as I placed the strip back on the heat. I dumped the mushrooms on two plates and handed the pink plate towards Maybelle.

She laughed as she saw it. "You know I would have eaten off of any plate, right? I don't care what it looks like." I stared at her in response. She smirked and stared back at me. She took her fork and extended it towards my plate. She picked up one of my mushrooms and opened her mouth to speak. "You know, you could have put less oil in the pan." I glared at her, threatening her with the prongs on my fork. Maybelle threw her hands up. "I was joking, ma'am!"

I rolled my eyes at her, setting my empty plate on the bottom of the sink. "You know, I thought the mushrooms could have been cooked for a bit longer."

Maybelle threw her head back and laughed. "You're funny."

I inspected her as I turned away from the sink. To my surprise, even without modifications, Maybelle looked relatively the same. Her hair was more obviously dyed; it was brassier without the help of the modifications and was more damaged with frizzy strands sticking out. The only other difference was her eyes. Naturally, they no longer had a pink tint to them.

I was bemused. Out of all Queens, I expected her to be modified the most.

Maybelle heard me walk away to leave. "Have fun, babe!" she exclaimed. She fixed her posture and wiggled her fingers to say bye to me.

She didn't bother to look at me.

Chapter Thirty-nine

It Smells of a Set-Up

I pushed the air out of my lungs. My hands were overly sweaty and felt large. I already knew I had long fingers, but my grip on my dagger made me feel like they were too long. I could feel every part of my hand and it was slightly uncomfortable. And damp from sweat. I cringed, rubbing the moisture off my dagger and onto my pants.

I pressed my eyebrows together as I stared at the window in front of me. Maybe the small dagger wasn't that good of an idea. I slid the dagger back into the center of the shield.

I inhaled as I slammed the edge of the shield onto the window and brought it back towards my face to brace myself from the falling glass. My breath hitched as I looked down at the shards around my feet. I hesitantly extended my leg to step onto the other side of the window.

Someone set Lauren up. Lauren was a clean lady obsessing to make sure everything was tidy. Her nose would wrinkle and she'd huff with her nose in the air if anything smelled slightly bad.

This house reeked. It couldn't have been Lauren's.

Come to think about it, the oddly put wood boards over her door weren't like her either.

However, I had to remember that this was no longer the

modified Lauren I was thinking about anymore. She no longer had Tech information to make her perfect.

I coughed. The house smelled of skunk and there was a strange humidity in the house. One wall was covered with a quilt. The same quilt Maybelle had on her couch. I sucked at my teeth. Was this Maybelle's doing? Burn marks covered one wall of the house. I looked back and noticed circular burn marks down the blanket and shook my head. *No way.*

But that wasn't the most surprising thing. The house was empty. Nothing was in this house. Nothing. There were four walls and no carpet. The flooring of the house was *dirt*. I walked on it. It was cushiony. I pressed my foot down harder on it. The dirt was all moist and stuck together. None of the dirt particles stayed on my shoes. I stomped on the dirt, two feet this time. The dirt sunk down like an elevator and sprung back up again. I clutched my arms in fear. I didn't want to risk seeing what was down there. For all I know, it would lead to my death. I looked down and exhaled slowly. I rubbed at my temples and looked back up.

The room started to burn my eyes and I squinted them to release some of the pain the smoke was causing. I shut my agape mouth. I didn't want to inhale whatever type of chemical was in this room either. I stepped out of the house, my eyes still wide open.

Someone *had* to have set Lauren up. No one had living conditions like this.

I stared at the house in front of me. Allison's. I walked towards it. Unsurprisingly, the door was locked.

I stared at the window.

"Mia," Maybelle's voice was stern. "Please don't do what you're thinking of doing." She laughed slightly at me and shook her head. "You're too curious for your own good."

She waited for me to walk up to her and rubbed my shoulder.

Maybelle spoke again. "Come here, I want to show you something." She leaned over to pick up more mushrooms from the burned planks of wood beside her house. She once again handed me the mushrooms and pointed to the wood. "That used to be my house!"

I looked at her in horror. "The one that was burned down like Nerissa's letter said?"

Maybelle scoffed, "You got it."

"Why did Marissa's siblings light the fire? They didn't have prejudices against *you*." I looked over towards Maybelle waiting for her answer.

Maybelle gasped in laughter. "People just love dramatizing stories don't they?" She looked over towards me and noticed my confused expression. She rolled her eyes before continuing. "No, Addy and Adaline didn't burn the house. They were wimps." She paused, debating on whether or not to continue. "Allison burned it. It was Allison."

Chapter Forty

It's a Lie

"Mia, you smell weird."

He was right I smelled of some sort of contaminated smoke.

Spencer's lanky arms were wrapped around my own and his head was right above my chest.

I chewed at my lip and leaned back. Spencer positioned himself so that his arm was wrapped around my shoulders. He rested his head beside the right side of my neck. "Yeah," I responded. "I went into Lauren's house. It reeked."

"Lauren's house?" He laughed. "Her house reeked?"

I sighed. *Of course, he didn't believe me.* "I don't think it's hers; it's just labeled that way."

He pointed to the trees behind us. "Lauren has a computer with modifications still. The trees are hyper-realistic. Only a good Tech could code that. She's probably using the house as a decoy to prove that the modifications took away the beauty of her house."

I repeated his words, "Only a *good* Tech?"

He immediately pushed down what I was thinking, "No. Not *that* weirdo. Do you seriously think *Kace* is smart enough for that?" He laughed in denial.

"He *is* smart. He's a good Tech." How could Spencer deny that Kace was skilled in what he does?

"The boy proposed that you distract Maybelle so that she'd start thinking that I escaped. How did he expect that to work?"

I scoffed at him, "Did you have any better ideas?"

He laughed at me, shocked that I was disagreeing with him. "Mia. You know I don't like arguing with people who aren't strong enough to have their own opinions. He's a go with the flow type guy and I don't deal with that." Spencer turned his head up slightly to see what I was thinking. "Come on, you're really upset over this? We just made up! We're finally friends again." He sighed, realizing that I wasn't going to respond. "I get it. You have a little crush on him." He paused, smiling smugly as he took in my silence. He scoffed, "Really, Mia? Him?" I looked down at him; he was smiling slightly.

"No. No crush. He's the only one who's supported me here and that's why we are *good* friends."

"Ouch!" Spencer gripped his chest dramatically. He then raised his eyebrows at pointed at me. "We not being friends during this *challenge* was on you."

"Why don't you say that again right before Courtney *murders* you?" I lamented.

Spencer groaned, flailing his right arm. "Why do you blame everything on Courtney? The prophecy is on a bunch of people. That sentence could have been about anyone."

"At this point you probably like Courtney."

Spencer let out a single laugh. "Mia, do you really think I *like* Courtney?" He raised his eyebrows. "I don't!" he exclaimed after seeing my expression. "I just want to escape! Mia. No, Mia. Stop making that face." I raised my eyebrows at him. He sighed, "You exhaust me, but I missed you."

He wrapped his arms around me again. He sniffled slightly until he left water on my shirt. I sighed letting him finish crying before speaking. "I'm coming with you. And then I'm coming straight back."

Spencer released his grip on me and leaned back, smiling. His tears were still damp near his chin.

Something was off.

Jesus.

I shifted my shoulder away from him.

He rubbed at his eyes, but his eyes weren't puffy from crying.

My breath was quickening. It was all an act.

His entire conversation was made so that I would say that. So that I would come with him.

He was acting. He was *manipulating* me.

Did he want me to protect him or something? That he'd be safer if I came with him?

Or did he have a plan with Courtney and wanted to kill me?

My legs quivered. I was suddenly cold. I brought my knees towards my chest and pulled them close.

Spencer's smile faded as he watched my expression turn into a scared one.

I gasped. "You have no emotions!"

Spencer's eye twitched. He sputtered before speaking. "You don't really think that. You don't think that I'm—that I'm some sort of—Mia. Mia. I meant what I said. I'm no *sociopath.*"

This was also a show. I scoffed, shaking my head. "I thought those tears were real, Spence."

"Mia!" He looked as scared as I was. "They were."

His face was washed out of color and his posture stiffened. He seemed more alert as he keenly watched me get onto my feet.

He was scared, but he sure as hell wasn't scared about losing me.

He was scared of the truth.

Chapter Forty-one

Never Put Your Back to Your Opponent

I caught a glimpse of recognizable caramel hair and orange eyes and I stopped dead in my tracks. Courtney was the kind of person you could pick out from a thousand people. She had bony arms, a thin smile, and an amazingly perfect posture. Her limbs were smaller than the rest of her fairly skinny body which made her look too fragile for her own good. Although, I never doubted she was weak. I didn't expect her to be outside her room. There was no way Courtney could escape from the door by herself. The only way she could escape without any outside help would be the elevator which let her outside, directly in High Tide. To escape from the interior of the Trap would require teleportation skills, which made it harder to return back to High Tide if need be. Someone had to have assisted Courtney out. And their presence still could be here.

I shivered as I pondered about how many people weren't able to get into Courtney's room and were trapped in this small entrance area. Once the challenge was over, they would die here with no access to food or water.

My breath quickened as I sat on the rocky and dirt-filled ground, behind a suitably large boulder. I rested my back against it in order to not be seen by Courtney or anyone who might have been here. The rock was brittle and a few pebbles broke away from the boulder whenever my finger touched it. I looked over at my hand as I pulled it away from the rock. There was a film of gray grease on my palms by a mixture of sweat and dirt that I hastily tried to wipe off on the sleeve of my shirt. I looked around at the environment, trying to calm my anxious breathing pattern. The room would have been pitch black if it wasn't for the small opening that allowed people in. I thanked myself for choosing to teleport rather than manually getting here because my fall would have definitely been heard by Courtney. With my back against the light escaping the entrance, I squinted to be able to see the detailing of the wall in front of me. The entire room was constructed with dark rocks, most of them had the same glittering specks on them which led me to believe they were all the same type of stone. There were a few scattered boulders near the one I was resting against and some were placed around the sides of the room as well. The area smelled of damp dirt to accompany the grime I was sitting in. There was no telling how long I've been in High Tide and my access to bathing was quite limited besides the occasional swims I took in the sea and the one shower I had at Maybelle's. So, I too was grimy. I wrinkled my nose as I squinted to look under my nails.

I paused, my finger close to my eyes as I was inspecting it when I heard the familiar squeakiness of Courtney's high-pitched-natured voice. It wasn't a sentence but more of a verbal gasp.

Another familiar voice started to speak, "The boy, Spencer. You know him and he doesn't want to be a King. Have you thought about helping him reach Earth again?" So there was a person that helped Courtney out of the room. I recognized the voice to be a female I knew, but I just couldn't put my finger on who it could be. The voice was deep and commanding but whose voice could it belong to?

"Since Mia and Maybelle are planning to make Mia Queen, would that mean I get a position as one as well?" Courtney asked curiously with a longing to her voice. My breath hitched at my own name.

"Yes," the woman's voice emphasized. Curious now of who this lady could be, I quickly looked at her to see who she was. *Allison.* I gasped quietly, then swiftly moved back to my original spot. It all started to make sense. Allison was trying to persuade Courtney to usher Spencer out of High Tide. She didn't want the competition. Allison continued, "It would."

If Courtney goes to Earth she'll bring someone. She's too afraid to go alone. She'll bring Spencer, I thought. *That was Allison's and Courtney's plan after all. Allison didn't want to risk her position as a Queen and Courtney was designed to harm those who came near the Trap.*

"You have a solid deal."

I hitched. I could have sworn the rock just moved.

Seconds later I was sprawling on my back and trembling because of the cold. The rock was now feet behind me. I furrowed my eyebrows. It was a huge boulder; it couldn't have moved.

"Ow!" I cried into the heavy, but crisp air. I sat up and grabbed my hurting arm. Luckily, it was my right arm that got hurt and not my left. I stared at my other, shaking hand waiting for my ability to work, but nothing happened. I tried again. Still nothing. *Your abilities don't work anymore, idiot.* My arm hurt. I prayed that it wasn't broken. I breathed out the air that I didn't realize I was holding. I laid on the rocky ground as the edges of the room started to get fuzzy.

A person whizzed past me. A black, felt mask was trying to slip off their face. I squinted in confusion. The person carried a large sack with them. I barely noticed. I was staring at my small feet, wondering if my new shoes got dirty from walking in mud. It started raining. Down pouring, actually.

The person broke something with a loud shatter. I looked up from my shoes.

I heard something and saw red. Stupidly, I walked into the house. A scream shocked through the house and I instantly ran towards it, recognizing my mom's voice. The last reddish-orange spark from the fire landed on my jaw, leaving a deep, but small gash. I cried, hard, griping on the burn on my jaw, until I heard *the sirens from police cars and fire trucks blow as the rain drenched the fire.*

It was burning hot.

The weather was freezing cold, actually, but it felt like my skin was melting off.

The heat was sharp. Painful.

And it burned. Quite literally.

I could recall the house that was in front of me anywhere.

"Hey, kid, you'll be fine." The cop spoke to me before turning back to his partner. "Just a couple of stitches should do it." He looked at me again, "Kid? Can you stand up? Can you hear me? Miss?"

The female officer coughed through the smoke as she turned to the man. "I think she's in shock, officer. Denial maybe— Miss? Can you comprehend what I'm saying?"

Dayton sounded stressed as he spoke, his voice shaky. "This is too complicated. Just pick her up."

The lady officer grasped me by my armpits to bring me inside her car.

She didn't let me in the ambulance.

Chapter Forty-two

Orange Blossoms

I didn't bother to move away from the door. It wasn't like I could find my way out anyway. I was very lucky that Courtney was in her room and Allison had just left. Otherwise, both of them would have heard me.

I heard the door slowly opening. I jumped out of the way, back towards the boulder. The metal door unlocked. A boy appeared. He was twirling keys held together by a ring between his fingers. Strung around the ring was a dog whistle and a pen.

He pulled his fingers up to fluff up his dark hair. His hair was obviously dyed; his brown roots peeked through the shade of black. He turned around to see if anything was behind him. I got a good look at his eyes. The whites of his eyes were tainted with bloody red veins. The skin around his eyes was purple. His skin had pinkish undertones that made him look sickly. He wrapped his fingers around the keys. His knuckles turned white and his blueish veins seemed to press against his skin. He rubbed the side of his forefinger to his lips. As blood started to rush up to his lips, his lips became a more pinkish shade than purple. The boy looked healthier than Courtney. Despite his sickish appearance, his bones didn't jut out of his skin.

He cleared his throat slightly as he slammed his elbow

against the door to warn Courtney that he was coming in. He stuck the first key into the keyhole and twisted it down. He stepped back slightly when he realized that Courtney was already at the door.

The boy tossed the keys up and caught them again before he dangled the keys in front of Courtney. The keys made a dainty clinking sound. The keys were unique. They were made of glass instead of metal and a flower was cut into the tops of both of them. The first key had an orange blossom design on it and the second a rose.

"Where did you get this?" The boy's voice was high-pitched to a point where it sounded whiny. There was something different in his voice. I frowned. He drawled his words. He had an English accent.

Courtney leaned over to snatch the keys from his hands. She was clutching the doorframe hard, her fingers straining. "This doesn't regard you." Courtney's voice sounded flatter than the boy's. "Did you get the information I needed from Lauren?"

The boy looked her up and down. His hands were still extended up despite the fact he wasn't holding the keys anymore. "I did."

Courtney waited for him to carry on. The boy didn't move. Courtney glared at him. "Carry on."

The boy chuckled and rested his elbow against the door-frame. Courtney seemed uncomfortable with their sudden closeness and moved back. The boy laughed again and looked down, his hair moving in front of his eyes. He looked up again. "You have to tell me who this *Spence* is first."

"He's escaping with me. He already told me. All you have to do is come with us, Andrew."

I exhaled. I remembered Andrew being Courtney's room-mate in her story.

Andrew looked at her. "And what after?"

"You go back to doing whatever illegal activity you used to do before you came here and you were supposed to ask Lauren where my family is."

Andrew's jaw clenched. "I didn't or will not do any illegal activity."

"Then why are you here?" Courtney huffed in aspiration.

"Cory. You're not letting me speak. Your parents are dead."

Courtney violently dropped her hands in annoyance. "You didn't even answer my—," Courtney paused. "What?"

"Your parents are completely dead. Dad from cancer and mom from diabetes-related issues. Natural causes." He paused. "I got Kace to list you as an emancipated minor. In two years you'll be of legal age anyway." Courtney reached for the edge of the door to shut it. Andrew slapped the door out of her way. "But you already knew that. You already knew your parents died. They died after releasing their position as Techs. They died before Lauren modified you."

"Leave me alone." Courtney's bottom lip quivered. Her face burned red and the skin between her eyebrows tensed up. She looked pissed.

Andrew looked tired. He used his shoulder and head to try and brush his hair away from his face. He didn't dare let go of the door. "You have no reason to escape, Cory. You have to tell me the truth."

Chapter Forty-three

Together

"Why are you pretending you want to escape? What are you doing, Cory?"

"It doesn't matter."

Andrew laughed. He was holding onto the door with every bit of strength he had. "You put on such a show. You acted like you didn't know they died! Do you want to be a Tech like your parents? Is that what this is all about?"

Courtney crossed her arms. "I want to be a Queen."

Andrew laughed once again, this time out of disbelief. "A Queen? One of those fakes? You're going to lose your future freedom on Earth to become one of those? Is it the immortality you want? Your brother is in a damn orphanage and you're worried about not living forever?"

Courtney gripped Andrew's shoulder. "He's not dead?" she questioned urgently.

"He's alive, yes." Andrew cocked up one of his eyebrows, curious as to how Courtney didn't know this. Andrew took in a deep breath. "He's got himself a girlfriend, but she's set to compete in the next High Tide Challenge."

"Which Queen is she related to?" Courtney's mouth barely moved as she spoke.

"Marissa. She's a *Neutral.* Whatever that means. Her name is Roxane, but she goes by the name Roxy."

She's like me. She's going to be a Neutral.

I was suddenly curious. I haven't met anyone else who had all of High Tide's abilities. I wondered how she would carry her power.

"She's like Mia."

Andrew tilted his head. "Who's Mia?"

Courtney dismissed him, her eyebrows furrowing as if she was in deep thought.

Andrew looked up and quickly let go of his grip on the door. "Kace said the computers were down, right?" Andrew turned towards Courtney.

"Yeah, there are no more modifications, if that's what you mean. Why?"

Andrew pulled Courtney's arm towards him. "I have a good feeling that crow is going to attack us."

Andrew shoved Courtney's head down as a bird swooped down towards her. Andrew jumped back as it slammed into the metal door. The bird collapsed causing a few black feathers to fly up towards them. The bird had a skinny head and legs. Its feathers seemed to be black, but its skin was a flaming red.

Courtney frowned. "I don't think that the bird was a crow. It looks like a vulture." The bird twitched. Andrew's breath hitched. "I don't think it matters, Cory."

The bird seemed to glitch. I squeezed my eyes shut as the bird started to glow a bright purple. A ray of purple extended up and Andrew reached his arm to his right to block Courtney from the light. The light died back down towards the ground and purple ooze seeped out of the bird. The bird squawked as it duplicated. The original bird remained the same, but the new one was a purple color.

Andrew flicked his hand back harshly hoping something would result from it. Andrew seized Courtney's hand to try and get her fire abilities to work. She snatched her hand back and glared at him.

I ducked down, facing the wall in front of me rather than Courtney's door. I rubbed at my closed eyes, watching colors appear in the darkness. I blinked them open, staring at the wall in front of me. I squinted. I slid down so that I was almost lying on the floor, my elbows propping me up. My feet were extended enough to reach the dirt wall. I kicked at some of the dirt. I gasped. The dirt was covering an old and soggy stone wall. A retaining wall. Retaining walls usually had water flowing through the bottom. I crawled forwards towards the wall and hoped neither Andrew nor Courtney could see me. I clutched my dagger and cut around a loose stone.

A dark figure rested its elbows on the boulder behind me. I resisted the urge to scream. I turned my head slightly. It was Andrew. He looked at me skeptically.

I pointed to the stone in my hands. Water split out and started to create a damp layer on the ground.

"You have to drown that," I motioned, with the rock, towards the bird who was pecking at Courtney's collar.

Andrew leaned forward towards me after nodding. He cupped his hands through the opening to try and push another rock out. His chest heaved as he forcefully pushed the stone away from the dirt. He took a second to breathe before reaching for another stone.

The water was unsatisfyingly warm. It was oddly thick too; mud had mixed in with the fresh water to create a fluid paste. Andrew wheezed in fatigue as he watched the water touch his thighs.

I looked at the bird. The vulture's twin moved a half step away from it at all times. Whenever the vulture moved the purple twin was right behind it. Courtney had the keyring with the glass keys and whistle in her hand and watched as the vulture struggled to stay up. Courtney had managed to sever the birds' wings. She looked down. The water reached inches above her ankles. She huffed and grasped one of the birds' feet and dragged them down. She fell forward as she pressed the dog whistle through the original creature's body. Air bubbles rippled the stillness of the water as the birds evaporated in her hands.

Courtney stood up slowly, still watching where the bird was. She was shivering. Andrew calmly walked towards her. Patches of dirt and shaved skin covered both his arms. His knuckles were skinned and bleeding. A drop of blood fell down from his forearm and towards the already soiled water. He moved his head towards Courtney's shoulder as if he was about to hug her, but instead, he extended his hand towards Courtney's. He peeled Courtney's fingers away from the keys. She willingly dropped the key ring set onto his palm.

He chuckled as he walked over to the boulder that I was leaning against. "Hi, Mia."

"I thought you didn't know who I was," I hissed. He was exposing me to Courtney. I clenched my hands.

"You aren't famous, but you are infamous." He cracked his neck before dropping the keys onto my lap. I squeezed my eyes shut as I watched the bird's internal fluids splatter onto my pants. I wishfully tried to rub the red away from my pants as I stood up. Andrew walked through the doors and seemingly disappeared as he walked into his own room. His voice extended from where he disappeared off to. "You're welcome, Mia!"

He knew I was hiding from the start. He pretended to not know of my existence to try to steer Courtney from thinking about me.

He was very smart. Emotionally smart.

I growled. Smart or not, he just exposed me to Courtney.

I tensed up, waiting for Courtney to scold me for stalking her.

There was a pause. I looked up. Courtney had extended her arms to ask for a hug. I leaned forward, hugging her with the left side of my body.

She whispered, "Why are you here?"

"I'm escaping with you. To make sure Spencer will be okay."

She smiled. "We have the same plan. Together we will come straight back."

I nodded. "That's the plan."

"They will never understand us, but together we will be Queens." Courtney reassuringly held my arm. Her hands were cold.

This wasn't real. Courtney was still modified.

Her hands were cold. Goosebumps followed wherever her hand touched my skin.

My hands were red and sticky. I dropped the keys into the water. My hands were sweaty.

Her hands were cold.

She was going to kill Spencer.

Chapter Forty-four

Lighter fluid

Allison's lighter was on the ground. The wrapping on the lighter was smooth and shiny. The deity Ares was depicted on the wrapping. He wore a warrior helmet and was holding something. I squinted to look at it better. Ares was holding a plant of some sort. A dainty leaf was depicted on it with white orange blossoms surrounding it. The stalk of the leaf held a withered orange with a triangle symbol on the center. Ares held the stalk above his head like the old orange was some sort of trophy.

I listened to the crack of the spark-wheel of the lighter as a yellow flame shot up.

Ares was always described in the presence of his flaming chariot; his fire a symbol of destruction and war. Hephaestus was also known for his fire; his fire was meant for building, for creating.

But neither of them were the gods of fire. A woman was. Hestia was one of the original twelve Olympian gods who vowed to keep peace at the Olympics. Hestia means "hearth" or "fireside". Because she was a pure and innocent virgin who had been given the centralized location in the home, her fire represented the hearth. And, also unlike the others, her fire was a symbol of peace. A symbol for togetherness.

Mcn are given the credit for what women do.

But we're not on Earth. We were in High Tide.

I valued the sense of woman empowerment here. Women were finally in strong positions of power, but what was the point of feminism when the Queens hated each other? What was the point of feminism if I hated Courtney? What was the point of feminism when women hate their fellow women?

Chapter Forty-five

Pessimists Don't Smile

I don't like it when Maybelle smiles.

She has a nice laugh and usually her laughs are genuine, but even then her laughs aren't as friendly as her smiles. Her semi-smiles usually engage only half of her mouth. Only one side of her lips would curve up. Her tongue would run across her teeth and she'd scoff.

But this smile looked too good to be true. All her perfectly white teeth were lined up perfectly in between her perfectly proportionate lips. Her cheeks were raised, causing the skin around her eyes to crease. Her body was relaxed as she effortlessly held up her body in the water by delicately holding onto the pier.

She looked optimistic. I wrinkled my nose.

Something was wrong here.

"Mia!" Maybelle had one of those smiles that curled up just enough to show the pink corner of her gums. "Get into the water!"

My pants were already dirty. The water would clean them. I debated getting into the water as I walked down the pier.

Maybelle playfully groaned loudly, rolling her eyes dramatically. "Stop overthinking things." She pushed herself higher through the water and grasped my right knee. With a laugh, she yanked me down. The front of my foot scraped against the edge of the pier.

I scrunched up my whole face as the stinging feeling of salty water shot up my nose. My arm hairs stood up in response to the cold water.

Maybelle's smile disappeared as she pulled up her hair to wring the water out. She rubbed her hands together and used her legs to kick so that she wouldn't sink deeper in the water.

Ringing. There was a distinct ringing.

I must have bit my tongue because I could taste metal.

Metal. I had just been pushed into the metal bar that held up the pier.

Breathe. There was a pressure in my chest and stomach asking me to breathe. My ears burned. My face burned. I wanted to press the cold seawater onto my face. I kicked at what was in front of me.

Maybelle was the person in front of me. Her hand was wrapped around my neck, pressing down on my larynx.

I wanted to scream. I wanted to feel the vibrations in my throat that came from speaking.

"What did you take?" Maybelle urged. "What did you take from Lauren?"

I clawed at her hand. Maybelle moved her hands to hold onto my shoulders so that I could speak.

Speaking never felt so good. "I didn't take anything," I rasped out.

The pressure in my stomach arose again as Maybelle pressed against my throat to push me into the water. I desperately wanted to push the carbon dioxide I had left in my lungs, but Maybelle's grasp made it hard to even breathe out. I flailed in the water.

Maybelle wouldn't kill me. She didn't have it in her to kill someone herself.

At least I hoped.

Her voice was muffled as she spoke through the barrier of water between us. "What did you take?"She yanked me back up into the air and let go of my throat, but I refused to speak.

I could hear the water in my ears and smell the water up my nose. I hated it.

"You need Lauren on your side, Mia. I need to know what you took."

I clawed at her, reaching for her skin with my nails. Her hand shook, debating on whether drowning me was worth it.

She huffed and hoisted me up onto the pier. I collapsed on the wood ground. I cupped my hands over my ears. I didn't want to hear the water that was stuck up them. I shook my head to try and get the fluid out. It didn't do anything.

I exhaled. I shouldn't have taken Kace's book and USB. *What am I going to do with the items anyway?*

Maybelle hopped onto the pier, walking over my extended arm. I listened to her heels click against the wood as she walked a bit farther than me.

Maybelle stopped walking, the clacking sound of her heels stopped. "Lauren isn't who you think she is."

Chapter Forty-six

The White in Orange, Orange in White

"Do you even know how to open a locked door?" I grunted, trying to use my dagger to pull against the door hinge. I took a second to pause, my dagger still lodged in the door. There was a faint mechanical whirring sound inside Allison's house. It made me want to break in even more now.

Spencer finally answered my question. "No. I have no clue." He stood behind me, his head cocked to his left to see what I was doing. He chewed at the inside of his cheek. He leaned forward, over my shoulder to reach for my dagger. He stepped slightly away from me to yank my weapon out. His hand wrapped around the hilt and he dropped it through the pocket on my shield. I stared at his hand as his knuckles went white from his grip on the doorframe. With his other hand, he shook the handle to the door. Surprisingly, the handle was weak and moved with his motion, making a repeating clicking sound as it moved up and down. Spencer turned his head towards me. "There's only one lock." He continued to hold eye contact before leaning back to press his shoe under the lock. The door shook back, the top of the door had moved away from the doorframe, signaling that it was barely broken. He sucked a breath in, lifting one of his feet up, debating on whether to try again. He pressed his foot into the concrete below us. The handle made a click sound again as Spencer pushed it down. His elbow rested to the left of the handle as he slammed the handle forward. The door swung open, crookedly leaning slightly upwards. The metal plate that once was on the side of the door was now in Spencer's hand.

I pivoted my shoulders to walk past Spencer to see the inside of the house.

I paused once my feet touched the inside of the house. I could feel the texture of the carpet through my shoes. Allison's carpet was soft and home like, the threads of the carpet stuck out and cushioned the ground. Maybelle's house had carpet, but the threads were knit together to create a flatter surface. I pressed my foot down against it, before speaking to Spencer who had stepped forward so that he was beside me and not behind me.

Spencer had already started to inspect the wall to our left. The walls in the house were painted a baby blue and plastic hooks were stuck to the upper parts of the walls. The hooks on the left wall were occupied with weapons. Swords and daggers were tied up and hung, shield straps strung over the hooks, and body armor rested against the wall.

I looked forward. A plastic cover with a gold padlock rested over something on the table in front of me. The cover was white and had a manufacturing line that exposed where the cover would split open if it wasn't locked. I stepped towards it. The whirring got louder. There was a computer in the cover. The table had drawers. I yanked at the gold knob on one of the drawers. The knob didn't budge. I reached for the knob again.

Spencer slapped my hand away. "Don't break that." He pointed to the keyhole next to the knob. "It needs to be unlocked. Try to find a key."

"That needs a key too," I stated, cupping my hand over the cover's padlock to Spencer. I shook the table. Something metal rattled inside. I turned to Spencer. "Do you think that's the key?"

He nodded, but he wasn't looking at me. His eyes lingered on my shield. "Give me that, Mia."

I looked down. "My shield?" Spencer nodded and so I handed it to him. He pulled out my dagger and compared it to his sword.

"They all have the same symbol," Spencer reflected. "They all have the same flower."

I walked towards him, reaching for the lighter in my pocket. "It's an orange blossom." I recalled my conversation with Allison. "Queen Allison said that orange was her favorite color. I didn't think that she would tell me that just for fun, so I put two and two together."

"Orange blossoms are white."

I glared at him. "Orange blossom. It has orange in the name. What flower do *you* think it is, then?"

"No. I got that," Spencer confirmed, seeming slightly annoyed that I wasn't getting what he was trying to say. "Orange blossoms are white."

I gasped. "You think the orange thing is a cover up. You think that this house is actually Lauren's." I remember being blinded by the lightness of the Tech building and the clothing Lauren made Kace wear. "That would make the house that's labeled as Lauren's actually Allison's house. It would explain the mess."

"Why else would there be a computer here? Have you seen Allison go into the Tech building?"

"Lauren has her own secret room in the building. I saw it. What's the point of that room, then?"

Spencer paused to think. "That room is too obvious. Plus it's clear she's trying to put the blame on Allison."

"What blame? It's a computer, that's it."

Spencer huffed, "A computer that has coded information about Marissa." Spencer gestured towards the direction of Marissa's bubble.

"Allison has a logical reason to have a computer. She has to make sure no one takes her place as a Queen. She would probably code something so that it's easier for her to fight against possible competitors."

Spencer's lips curled upwards. "By possible competitors, you mean me."

My voice softened. "Yeah."

"No matter who it is, someone planned for you to do something to the computers. Someone thought that you were going to use the computers to your advantage."

"I didn't use the computers to my advantage," I declined. "Kace already promised me that he was going to steer his monsters away from me."

Spencer's eyebrows furrowed at Kace's name. "Of course he did." Spencer chewed the inside of his cheek. "Well, if you didn't use the computers to assist you then why did you disconnect them?"

"I guess I was curious. I wanted to see if she'd be different. If she'd finally become human."

"By 'she' you mean Courtney," Spencer stated and I nodded in return. "Whatever, Mia. Let's find the key."

"I just don't understand. Why would a group of adults host an event where children fight against them and then modify a child to fight against these children as well? It doesn't make sense."

Spencer ignored me. "Mia. We need to find the key to the drawer."

I nodded and pointed at the table. A plastic plant with a white, ceramic pot stood on the wood of the table. The plastic dirt didn't connect to the edge of the pot. The dirt looked separate from the pot, almost as if I could pull the plastic and dirt duo out of the pot.

I leaned forward to grab the pot. I shook the pot upside down, and to my surprise, the dirt didn't move.

Spencer stared at the plant. "Allison wouldn't make it that obvious."

I huffed, inspecting the dirt around the plant. The plastic leaves felt smooth and cold. I grabbed the faux tuft of leaves and yanked it out.

A metal key rattled onto the floor.

"There's no orange blossom on it," Spencer said, ignoring the fact he was wrong about the key.

I held my breath as I inserted the key into the rusted keyhole. The key slid in perfectly. Squeezing my eyes shut, I twisted the key.

"Mia." My breath hitched as Spencer extended his arm to push me back. The drawer box had broken and fell right below my feet. Spencer gasped out, before kneeling to see what was in the drawer. Spencer placed three things on the table: another key and two cards made of plastic. He lifted one of the cards. It was a school ID. "Roxanne M. Corbyn." The girl in the photo looked around my age. She had long, but thin brown hair. Her big eyes offset her long face and nose. She had long brown lashes that complimented the dark hazel color of her eyes. He picked up the second one. "Colin I. Meyer."

I froze. "That's Courtney's last name."

I studied the picture. He had the same round lips as Courtney and matching blonde hair that looked orange where the light hit it. He had a weak jawline, but a strong cheekbone structure. His hair covered his eyes. "They look so similar," Spencer remarked.

I picked up the key from the table. The whirring sound from the computer rang in my ears. I quickly twisted the key.

The case split in half. As suspected, there was a computer with a worn down keyboard next to it.

A sticky note covered part of the computer and Spencer shifted in front of me to peel it off. He took a deep breath before reading what was on it out loud. "Property of Kace Striker."

Property of was written by someone with average handwriting and Kace's name was scrawled out with his messy signature.

I looked away and reached for the mouse to turn on the computer. I didn't want to think about what that meant.

Spencer grabbed my arm. "Do you know what this means? Kace is behind all this. He expected you to unplug everything, so that he wouldn't get in trouble. When you met him in the room he didn't fight you, right?"

I let out a breath as my hand shook. Spencer's arm was still clutched on my arm. "Not really." I swallowed down the lump in my throat.

Spencer nodded and then snickered. "I can't believe he's behind all of this. What would his motive even be?"

My stomach churned. *I should have known. I should have known.*

Spencer opened his mouth to speak again, probably to poke fun at Kace, but immediately shut his mouth after seeing my expression. He turned back to the computer to power it on.

Blueprints. The computer's home screen was a layout of High Tide. The Tech room rested against the east boundary. The sea surrounded the south side. To the west was the woods where Lauren gave me a letter. We were southwest where all the houses were. A black circle marked the Trap which was northeast. My eyes flickered to the side of the map. A separate map marked the interior of the Trap. Half of it was Andrew's room and the other was Courtney's.

Courtney's room.

My hand cupped over my mouth. "It's a wall. It's a wall."

Spencer looked worried; he studied the map and looked back at me, trying to see what my realization was. "What's a wall?"

I pointed to Courtney's elevator. "There's no door symbol."

Spencer's jaw dropped. "Courtney never had an entrance to High Tide."

My chest heaved as I gasped at Spencer. "Her story was fake. I was right this whole time."

Chapter Forty-seven

Bricks

The elevator doors opened painfully slow. The button to my right glowed white to match the arrow pointing up above the lift. I refused to blink as I watched the set of doors creak as they barely pulled away from each other. I furrowed my eyebrows as I clasped the edge of the left door. I strained the muscles in my arm to try and push the door to make it move along faster.

I didn't have time for this.

I gasped. The back of my hands felt something scratchy. The opening was too dark to see through it, so I glided my hand back in the crevice. My thumb grazed the soft, almost squishy feeling of a type of glue. My fingers brushed the scratchy, coarse structure of the wall next to the elevators. It didn't matter that what made the structure, but the fact there was one.

The hairs on my neck stood up as hot air brushed it gently. A cold hand clasped my shoulder and yanked me back.

The elevator door was finally open, exposing the red bricks behind.

"Don't you see Courtney? They lied to you." I turned around me to see Courtney. I furrowed my eyebrows. I couldn't tell what she was thinking. "The story that you remember so well is fake."

Courtney gave me an incredulous look, her eyebrows raised and mouth dropped. "Then *who* modified me, Mia?"

I rubbed the side of my forefinger against my bottom lip. "Your parents were Techs. They brought you here for a reason."

Courtney laughed in disbelief, her laughter turning into a scoff. "My parents? Then why is my brother an orphan, hmm? He could have been modified too. Mia, I'm just like you. I'm one of you. I'm a High Tide Kid."

"Courtney."

"No," she shook her head. "They-my parents-could never. That's inhumane. That's not normal. I'm not like that. That's not in my blood, Mia." She paused, studying my shock at her outburst. "Mia. I'm just like you. I'm you. We are the same."

"If you're not modified, then I have a question for you," I said, sucking my teeth. Courtney's face relaxed, hoping that I believed her. She nodded. "Why do you want to go to Earth? You know Spencer is going to die there if he listens to you. So why do you want him to die?" I pressed my lips together as Courtney's breath hitched.

"Look, I need to see it. I need to see Earth one last time before I become Queen. Because then I'll never see it again. He's the first competitor that is giving me this opportunity and, Mia, I need it. And even if he does—even if he dies, he'll be written in history. He'll be the first person to escape."

"You're acting like he's a news article!" I exclaimed.

"Mia, you can't live your life based on a piece of *poetry* claiming that someone's going to die. Lauren wrote that prophecy, not some mysterious force. Lauren! He's not going to die."

Courtney was taller than me. Only by a few inches, but today she seemed to hover over me. She always had a sense of maturity over me, like Kace did, since he was older as well. I felt small.

I listened to the sound of both of us breathing. "How old are you, Courtney?"

Courtney dropped her shoulders, happy that the subject was changed. "Sixteen. Nine when I came here."

Nine.

Chapter Forty-eight

The Future

"If anything happens, you will take my place."

I watched as my hair tie fell out of my hand and plopped into the water. "What?"

"I don't want anything going wrong when you replace Marissa, since she's in that state. So I'm leaving my position."

"You can do that?" I didn't want to ask why she was willing to do so. When Maybelle chooses to be kind, it's best to let her come to her own conclusions.

"Yes. I will lose my immortality state. Not that it matters because the computers are down. Not a big deal."

"And you won't have control over anyone," I added.

Maybelle growled under her breath, "That is true."

"You're not doing this for Marissa. You just don't want Courtney to take your place."

"Courtney is not a High Tide Competitor."

"Tell that to Allison, because she seems very determined to—"

Maybelle interrupted me. "Allison has no idea what she's doing. You will take my place. That is final."

Maybelle used her arms to push herself off the dock. She treaded water to reach my hair tie and dropped it in my hand.

Maybelle placed her elbows on the dock, splashing me slightly before speaking again. "You can leave now."

Chapter Forty-nine

Running Away
Solves Everything

I realized, standing in front of the two of them, I've never personally seen Spencer and Courtney interact.

They stood close together. Too close. Andrew sat on Courtney's bed, his teeth clenched slightly.

Andrew sighed in relief, "You're finally here." He looked behind him, towards where the hallway intersected between his room and the door to Earth. "Let's go."

Courtney looked at Andrew. "Spencer already looked at the door. There's a combination lock. He's going to try to break it. Mia and you can make sure no one walks in."

Andrew looked to me for confirmation. I shrugged.

"Perfect," Spencer concluded.

I sat next to Andrew.

I inhaled, cracking my knuckles to the sound of Spencer clicking away at the combination lock.

Andrew turned his head towards me, his eyes lingering on my knuckles. He watched as my fingers pressed down on them to create the cracking sound that was filling the room.

I could hear Andrew swallow before he spoke. "You feel threatened by silence, don't you?"

I frowned. "I don't feel threatened by silence. I'm just nervous about leaving."

"You chose to come with us. You don't have the right to be nervous."

I stood up. "What kind of statement is that?"

"Mia," Spencer chided, not looking away from the lock.

I could barely see Spencer since he was down the hallway. I could only see part of his hair and the white short sleeved shirt he had on. It was sweat soaked and he kept trying to pull it away from sticking onto his skin.

I sat back down, listening to the metal of the lock whirring. A *clink* signified that Spencer had gotten it to open. I heard Courtney sigh.

Andrew grabbed my shoulder as we jumped at an unfamiliar sound. I pulled out my dagger at the direction of the door.

"Run!" Andrew exclaimed, hoisting me up and pushing me towards the door. Spencer slipped out first. Courtney was right behind him.

"Guys, let's think through our decisions," Lauren's voice was calm. She was acting as mediator.

Pretending to act as a mediator.

My heart raced at the sound of a gun being loaded.

Andrew shut the door behind us, panting.

The world was spinning.

I coughed at the air. It was too cold to breathe in. I collapsed onto Andrew, who was also struggling to catch his breath.

My fingernails dug into his skin as we both sputtered out breaths.

Chapter Fifty

Blood in a Bottle

Blood. There was blood everywhere.

I could sense the blood, almost smell it. It filled the bodies that stood beside me. And with one movement, the contained blood would spill.

Andrew's watch said it was Noon. It definitely wasn't Noon. It was dark out but light enough to still see the clouds forming above us. I was guessing it was around eight o'clock.

"Where are we?" Spencer stood beside me, his shoulders tensed up. He wore a gray Henley shirt and was tugging at the collar. Beside him stood Andrew, who was picking at his nails. He pulled up his sweatshirt hood over his knit hat. Courtney was wearing the same deep purple, puff-sleeved shirt that she was wearing the day I met her. She was standing oddly close to me, her arm brushing mine.

I pointed out into the far distance. "That's the London Bridge."

Spencer squinted, waiting for his pupils to dilate, to see it better. "Tower Bridge," he corrected.

Andrew nodded. "What he said. At least we know our location."

Blood. My heart beat faster. The adrenaline swam through the blood.

I dug my nails into Spencer's skin. His skin looked red. Blood red.

He shook away from me. "There's nothing to be afraid of, Mia. We're free."

I winced as a pair of hands pushed my arms together and pulled me back. I squatted on the ground, still feeling the pain from the hands.

My ears rang. I covered them and brought my knees to my chest.

Andrew's knees collapsed as he fell backward. Backward into Spencer's hands. Spencer's knuckles turned white as he struggled to hold him up.

There was blood. And it poured out awkwardly, soaking into the layers of Andrew's clothes.

Clink. Clink.

She missed. Lauren missed.

No, she didn't miss. Andrew saved him.

Andrew saved Spencer.

His black sweatshirt darkened as it was dampened. It seeped down into his shoulder in a claw-like motion.

Spencer had dropped Andrew carelessly on the ground, Andrew's limp arms flung haphazardly over his body. The blood, making his lips pink, sucked out of his skin.

Was Spencer worth saving? Andrew wasn't supposed to die; he wasn't written in the prophecy, but here he was: cold and on the ground.

A tear fell down as my cheeks burned. I turned towards Lauren, my shoulders crossed.

Andrew didn't deserve to die.

I watched as Lauren's fingers quivered near the trigger.

I watched.

Clink. Clink.

Chapter Fifty-one

Roxanne M. Corbyn Won't Tell an Adult

Nerissa reflects on her realization that High Tide was created to teach humans the importance of history, stating that, "We live on Earth to realize what we did wrong. We live in High Tide to fix our mistakes."The letter she had sent that contained these words allowed me to prepare for the mental labor of dealing with High Tide. Evidently, Nerissa made me a better person. The girl who first stepped foot into High Tide was a spitting image of Maybelle. Or wanted to be like Maybelle. But now I knew I wanted to be nothing like her.

However, the alikeness of Maybelle's and Nerissa's rage tendencies were uncannily reflected in Courtney.

I read somewhere that we can't create something we haven't seen before. The Tech that modified Courtney had to be inspired by Maybelle; their similarities were too close. I needed to be wary of Courtney and the tendencies she could have. I remembered her face when she had a knife to my throat. I rubbed at the puffy mark that it made. I had the right to be scared of Courtney because this was all her fault, but her bubbliness, loving nature, and possibly a small attraction made me wish I knew her under different circumstances. But what if she never had a personality; was it all just modified in her?

I wanted to hate her; I really did. I looked over at Courtney, whose hand was covered over her mouth. The skin around her eyes was red. This was all her fault. She was the one who brought Spencer here. She was modified to kill him.

The more I stared at him, the bluer his face looked. Spencer's lungs were what took the most impact from Lauren's bullet and that was depicted on his face. The veins under his skin puffed out under the paleness of his skin.

Courtney's dry skin scratched against my own. She squeezed my wrist. "Get rid of the satchel."

I stepped backward and thanked God that it was dark out.

"Excuse me, Ma'am. Do you need me to call the police?"

I resisted the urge to scream. I turned around, my fingers over my lips. A girl, a bit younger than me, stood silently. She had masculine arms and a strong back, but she was short. Her hair reached to her waist gently. She had frail hair that looked light on her head.

My throat seemed to close up. I couldn't believe I was talking to someone on Earth. I was talking to someone new. "No. Don't bring the police, I'm not pressing charges." I paused to look down at my bag. "What's your name? Where do you live?"

She frowned, confused about why I was asking that question. "Roxanne, people call me Roxy. I live in Westminster."

"No, you don't. You live down the street." I gestured my chin towards the apartments nearby. There was no way she was traveling that far away from her home at her age and at this time.

She nodded reluctantly. "Why do you ask?"

I pulled the satchel off from my shoulder. I sighed in relief that the codebook wasn't pushing down at my shoulder anymore. "You need to bring this to an adult. This has important information. Bring it to someone who knows computer science."

She heaved as her shoulders dropped, not expecting my bag to be heavy, and nodded.

Roxy wasn't going to bring the book to an adult. I could sense it. I sighed.

But there was no way I could bring the book to someone this late, there was no one else on the streets.

I felt my chest cave in as I heard Lauren's voice echo through the passageway to the Trap. "You two are very lucky."

I turned around swiftly to look back at Spencer. His green eyes seemed to dim into a hazel color and the blood that brought color to his face drained down, susceptible to gravity.

I looked down at Courtney's feet. "'Lucky.' What did she mean by that?"

"Well, she obviously didn't murder us. I'd call that lucky," Courtney seethed. I gasped. Courtney never made sly remarks. She was always kind, even if you knew she was faking it. My fingers rested over my slightly ajar mouth. Courtney scoffed, "Oh, don't be surprised. You had to have known that whole happy-all-the-time thing was fake, right?" I swallowed. "Come on, you were the only one who believed I was modified." I looked back down. I always thought she was modified, but I believed that if the modifications went away she'd be more genuine. I would have never thought that her friendliness was modified too.

"Well, then, are you still modified?"

She grinned at me and tugged at the skin behind her ear. She pulled part of her hair up so I could see the technology that was stuck in her skin. The piece was skin-colored and when she yanked it out, a needle was stuck to it. I watched as the new gash in her skin dribbled out blood. I held my breath. "It doesn't work on Earth," Courtney stated. "And

Earth is the only place I can pull it off." She tossed the piece on the floor and stepped on it. "And now, it will *never* work."

I gripped my head in my hands, pressing my fingers onto my scalp. It all made sense. Courtney needed to go to Earth to get rid of the piece that was controlling all of her actions.

But that also meant that *someone* was controlling her.

I rubbed my hand against my shoulders, feeling my muscles slightly relax under my touch. "Who has the other piece?"

She laughed and her mouth and teeth seemed to glow. She was smiling in a new way I haven't seen before. The corners of her lips extended up and her teeth were placed perfectly near her bottom lip. "Don't you know, Mia? Who else could it be?"

I squeezed my eyes shut as my whole body seemed to ache. I felt like I was going to pass out. "He lied to me. Kace told me he had no connection with you anymore."

Courtney inhaled, mid-laugh, "You think he'd be honest about that? He wanted you to like him. Of course he was going to make himself look better." She leaned towards me, "Would you tell him if it was the other way around?"

I blinked. "No."

"Exactly." Courtney extended her hand, palm up, asking me silently to take her hand. I glided my fingers onto her palm but quickly retrieved them, suddenly aware of the awkward contact we made. She eyed me with a perplexed look. I walked alongside her towards the entrance to the Trap.

I jogged up to her. "Are you not upset about Andrew?"

She sharply irked, "It's not my problem. I can't do anything about it."

I scoffed, "He was your friend."

Courtney scoffed back at me, "What friend? I was modified since I knew him. If I ever said the two of us were friends, that wasn't me."

"He cared about you," I mumbled.

"Well, I don't see you crying. What happened to the whole 'I'm going to save Spencer' gig or was that just your savior complex coming out?" Courtney accused.

I looked down. "I don't have a savior complex; I just wanted to do whatever I could and I couldn't save him."

"Sure," Courtney nodded and turned to walk away from me. "Good luck, Ms. Savior," Courtney deadpanned.

Nerissa might value the idea of accepting our past. But the past repeats itself. That past becomes our future.

Chapter Fifty-two

Trash Day

Clammy. That was the word. My hands felt clammy. My body felt clammy. I didn't feel right. The death was expected, but it didn't feel right. The distance in my friendship with Spencer made the situation easier to handle. Spencer never loved me as I did him, as if he were my own blood. But, Spencer wasn't the type for showing emotions like me. He knew words that made sentences that made me re-think things. "You can't live like this," he said. But I could live like this. I had been living and staying that way in High Tide. Without him. I've learned to be independent, so why did it feel like I was missing something inside?

It might have been because of my guilt about the way I treated him in High Tide, but he wasn't the kindest to me either. Or maybe it was that he was never there for me when I needed him. He wasn't even willing to share the thing he knew about my mother's murder, even though he knew when he left High Tide he'd never see me again. He knew how important that was to me.

High Tide was shaky today; some sort of fearful energy caused my knees to wobble. I stared up at the junk pile that once was the tech building. The walls that hoisted up the building were slabs of wood that weren't even sanded down.

My shoe sunk down into a muddy spot on the ground as I stepped in.

Lauren sat on the ground, her legs elegantly folded beside her. She had sturdy legs like it would take a good force to knock her off her feet. Her midfoot curved gently to rest on the slanted heels on her brown sandals. Covering part of her shoes was the A-line skirt of her pale pink dress. The skirt was split into threes, one part covering her shoe, the other flowed over her knees, and the last allowed her to sit on the fabric. She still looked proper and clean despite the dirt that pressed against her dress. It was the first time I'd seen her in anything but white. She still looked pretty too. Her brush slid down her new fluffy brown hair that carefully framed the round features on her face. Lauren had used her ability to modify herself to an extreme. She fixed herself up with sharper features and stick-straight hair, but it never looked natural. And I guess she never wanted to look natural; she just wanted to appear the way her self-imposed beauty standards wanted her to look.

I had to admit, without the modifications, she didn't look like herself.

With her middle and forefinger, she extravagantly pushed strands of hair away from her face, as if she was putting on a show. She pressed her fingers against her lip to rub away excessive lipstick. "You're damn lucky that Allison had another computer," Lauren commented, still working to blend the color on her lips. "How else would you assume we get oxygen while being underground, Mia?"

I blinked. She had a point. I tugged at my shirt, uncomfortable with the way the fabric rested on my back and the buttons probed against my skin.

"Actually, I was hoping to run into Kace," I pointed out.

Lauren leaned forward to look through a gold compact mirror, brushing at the lipstick that smudged away from her lips. The mirror case was textured with vines and tree leaves extending to the center that highlighted the painted white petals of an orange blossom. She looked at me through the reflection from her mirror. She hummed slightly and gestured for me to sit down next to her. She shut the mirror with a hollow snap. "Let me tell you a story, Mia."

Chapter Fifty-three

The Day the Widow Dies

A pale woman sat down in front of the desk, her hands wobbling despite her grip on the armrest. She had blonde hair that had a bevel at the tips. A band wrapped around her ring finger. She reached to the back of her head to push her hair to her right shoulder. She wore a flowy, cream halter top and faded jeans. A woman reached forward and rested her hand on the nape of her neck. With her pointer finger, she pulled at the dainty chain around her neck.

The woman looked mid-age with deep sunken skin that pulled her skin into her bone structure, leaving impurities on her face. She had tribal braids woven into her hair that pulled it back, exposing her jut-out bone structure. When she reached her hand up to study the locket on the chain, her dress hiked up slightly. It was a thick red material that was cut out to have a sweetheart neckline. The dress fell to her ankles, slightly exposing a pair of Mary Janes. She opened the locket as she swung it back and forth in front of her own face.

"Could I please have that back, Allison?" The woman had a deep voice that seemed to command Allison what to do, despite her not having any clear hierarchy in this situation. If Allison was anything, she wasn't as mature as this lady.

Allison was different. Older, probably in her forties. I hadn't thought about the idea that she was heavily modified too.

Allison leaned forward, resting her elbows on the lady's shoulders. The locket remained open and now was in front of the woman's face. "Mrs. Meyer, or should I say miss?" The woman didn't move, yet still gripped onto the chair. Her nails cut through the soft, leather fabric. "Is this your daughter?"

"Yes."

"Where is she?"

"Lauren has kept her in the detainment."

Allison gasped mockingly, "And her crime?"

"Innocence."

"Well, then, should we work towards replacing her with her brother?"

"No. Courtney will remain in detainment."

Allison pouted. "That's not enough, Miss Meyer."

"I will not have my daughter become one of those things."

Lauren laughed slightly, listening to what she said as she stood at the doorway. She had some of her softer features, but her hair was her infamous light and pin-straight hair. She slipped on a white jacket. The jacket had a strip of fabric with button clasps that hung down to her thighs. "She's going to be much more, Mrs. Meyer. I'll assure you." Lauren walked over to the edge of the desk and propped up her laptop. "And I'll also assure you that you are currently in a position where I have more power over you." She pulled the laptop towards the lady. "So, out of the kindness of my heart, I'll give you two options. You can either code your daughter yourself or you can write your death day on your file."

The laptop had the lady's name, birth info, and characteristics. The lady leaned forward studying the information. Next to the slot that laid an empty death information box, she typed the date that was on her watch.

Mrs. Meyer hit the save button.

Chapter Fifty-four

All Hail the Two New Queens

"You're saying that's what you did to Kace."

"Exactly. I'd say I was much kinder to him than I was to Spencer, wouldn't you say so?"

"I can't believe you took all that effort to get rid of him. He wasn't even a threat to your position as Queen."

Lauren reached her arm up to rest her fingers on my shoulder. She looked up from under her lashes. "Mia, don't you see? This is what Maybelle asked for. This was *her* plan. She didn't want him to take her place."

I shook my head. "No. She thought Courtney was going to get rid of Spencer, not you."

"Maybelle wanted Spencer dead. She got Spencer dead."

"But that didn't even worry her at the moment. Allison told her that Courtney was going to take her place. She should be worried about Courtney, not Spencer."

"Oh my!" Lauren gasped to let a laugh in. "You really don't know anything do you? Courtney's immortal. She can't die."

"Excuse me?"

"We've already prepared for you and Courtney to become Queens. You two are already Queens." Lauren sighed, "It's a shame. Do you know how bad I wish I could have killed you? You made me kill him, my only Tech. He was completely pure and you *soiled* him."

I scoffed, "Me? You were the one who wanted Courtney modified and Kace did that. He did what you wanted."

Lauren brought her hand down to her chest as if she was surprised about what I said. "You think *I* wanted Courtney to be modified?" Lauren gasped. "I just wanted Courtney to be like the other monsters. I never wanted her to be a *hitman!*"

"Then, who?"

"Allison has a computer in her house. We agreed that we would hide one there in case anyone impulsive like you came around. Access to food, water, and oxygen were all coded in that specific computer. Courtney was originally coded in the computer in my office, but Allison found *flaws* in her design.

"Courtney wasn't able to recall events in her life. Her memories were erased, and thus she had no emotions regarding what happened in her life. So, Allison had to recode them back into her. Sure, there are some flaws, but it is much better than it was before. But that gave her intuition. She's smarter than ever before."

I pressed my lips together. Courtney's confusion regarding her memories and the fact she would remember things that never existed were explained through Lauren's theory.

I frowned. Lauren had somehow shifted all the blame from herself onto Allison. I recalled Maybelle blaming Allison for setting her house on fire. Could all of this actually be Allison's fault?

Both of the people I trusted had their stories wrong. Kace told me he reported to Lauren when in reality he was Allison's Tech.

Nerissa wrote that Marissa's sisters were the ones who burned Maybelle's house. She stated that Marissa's sisters were the reason for Maybelle's and Marissa's feud. But, May-belle told me Marissa and she were friends. So was there a feud in the first place or was that just the way Nerissa told their story?

I still had Lauren's note. How could I tell if the infor-mation on that sheet of paper was factual if she wrote the prophecy herself? How could I know if she was just playing with my emotions?

I bit my lip recalling the prophecy. *Edited girl.*
Edited.

Meaning that the person who was edited changed herself. Change was not by the force of another being. I looked down at Lauren, who continued to brush her hair. "The prophecy was never about Courtney. It was about *you*. About how'd you be the death of Kace. Not Courtney being the death of Spencer. I got the whole thing wrong. You're the edited girl."

Lauren grinned, rubbing at her bottom lip. "You finally got it."

"But then what were the other sentences about, since you wrote them yourself? *You* can't predict the future."

Lauren smacked her lips. "No. No, I can't. I gave you the prophecy after all the other Kids died. I already knew what happened to them."

"You planned to kill Kace? And why would you warn me?"

"Kace had already had an infatuation with you. He planned to steer monsters away from you while Spencer fought twice the amount he was supposed to. I'm surprised he was so easy to kill; the kid is resilient."

That's the Spencer I know.
Knew.

Lauren continued. "Any how, the way Kace spent so much time designing those beasts only to not put them to the use they were supposed to have—there was no use for him anymore. And don't you think I knew he was supporting Allison? It was so obvious," she huffed, "obvious to everyone, but you. Didn't you see Kace's constant need for positivity in Courtney? You do really think someone like her would be overwhelmed with happiness?" Lauren fluffed up the sides of her hair. "I thought you were smart. You were supposed to get the prophecy thing right away. And I expected you to worry about Kace like you did so with Spencer. You were so stupid, but it was entertaining. You had the totally wrong idea, but the same outcome: anxiety."

I looked down, upset with myself. I sniffed, "Where's Kace?"

Lauren blinked. "Dead."

"No, I meant where is his body?"

"Where do you think?"

I nodded. I had a good idea. I paused before speaking again. "If both Courtney and I are immortal and waiting to become Queens, why hasn't the challenge ended yet?"

"The challenge doesn't end until the bomb lights."

"And where do I find the bomb?"

Lauren smiled deviously. "I can't wait for you to find out."

Chapter Fifty-five

Cold

A fist slammed into the carpet. "Mia," Kace winced. His skin was scaling and purple bruised specks covered the reddened areas of his skin. One of his hands was gripped onto his rib as he gasped for breath.

My fingers brushed my lips. "Kace?"He swallowed, lifting part of his back up. I knelt down to him. He looked terrible. The whites of his eyes were now red and his lips were purple. He reached up to grab onto my elbow. "I only have the energy to say this once, Mia." He peeled his hand away from his side to pull it up to his ear. In his fingers laid an exposed earpiece that matched what Courtney had. "Step on it."

I frowned as I held the piece. "You said you had nothing to do with Courtney."

Kace exhaled. "I never meant to hurt you. I just—I just wanted them to like me. I wanted to be as impressive as one of them. They always wanted something out of me, even after I did what they asked. But look where that got me." He let out a painful laugh.

I knelt back down. The earpiece Kace had was now bent. I chucked it across the room. "How are you not dead?"

"I coded that I died out of poisoning," he coughed and rolled over to his side. He tried to laugh, but it came out more like a sputter. "That was a bad idea. I didn't think it would hurt this bad." He pulled out a piece of paper. "I don't have the energy to verbally explain this, but I wrote this note." He leaned forward to look me in the eyes. "If you—when you—find a way to code your mom back to life, bring me back." He looked down, a tear threatening to fall from the water collecting in his eyes. "I don't want to die." He pressed his fingers against my back, offering me a lopsided hug. I rested my chin on his neck and stared at Allison's computer to try and distract myself from him.

To distract me from his inevitable death.

And I hugged him until I felt him go cold.

Chapter Fifty-six

The Art of Missing People

Hey Mia,

The USB attached that's labeled as "M" has information regarding your mom. It's a file with collective information regarding her looks, birth, important information, and personality. USBs A and B have similar information regarding both Spencer and I. They're formatted differently because they're used as the plugs that activate the bombs. This will all make sense soon enough. I didn't clarify which USB is Spencer's and which is mine. It's your choice whose USB you want to ruin by using it for the bomb. I made them anonymous in hopes that if you don't use mine, you'll bring me back like you'll do so with your mom.

I hate doing this and the last thing I wanted to do was put pressure on you, but I did this out of greed. I admit it.

I'll miss you, Mia.
No pressure of course,
KS

Kace's handwriting was scrawled haphazardly across the paper, going against the rules of lined paper. But the back of the sheet was carefully designed. A drawing covered the back of the paper, the lines that Kace avoided when writing supported his drawing.

It took me a while to recognize myself in his drawing. My hair fell down to my shoulder blades. I was sitting in a chair with one leg extended out and one leg close to my chest. I wore flowy pants and a tucked in shirt that was darkly shaded. My face wasn't completely visible because I was looking down at my hands. One hand held my leg and the other was holding my dagger.

The dagger was pointed towards myself.

Chapter Fifty-seven

Burned Houses
Are Still Homes

Maybelle always seemed like a different person in the comfort of her own home. As if she was given the freedom to act the way she wished to rather than the way that was expected of her. Despite her sarcasm and crude personality, she seemed softer when she was at home.

If I lived here, would this home do the same for me? I tapped my foot on Maybelle's carpet as I frowned recalling Elaine. If anything, Spencer felt more comfortable in her home as opposed to my own comfort in that house. I winced as I thought about Spencer.

Sure, I felt a bit guilty about Spencer's death and I sure didn't want to think about his death, but it wasn't nearly as bad as I expected it to be when I read Lauren's prophecy.

I found my old clothes still sprawled out the same way they were before. Maybelle hadn't bothered to touch them. She gave me my own space, not really caring what I did in her house. I scoffed; she was the complete opposite of Maybelle. I picked up the pants. My fingers picked up Lauren's note.

I brought the note up to my face. "Speaking of the devil," I murmured to myself. "I need to read Lauren's note."

The High Tide Challenge was ending; Lauren didn't want me to read the note right away during the challenge, but if I opened it up any later it would have been too late.

In letting go, we find. Good luck, Mia Lopez -Marissa King.
I frowned. *What the heck?*

I looked back up at the jacket next to the pants. Kace had pulled together the entire outfit. I half-smiled, remembering our conversation. I walked into the bathroom. I scrunched up my hair to pull it through a hair tie, sighing at the relief of fresh air against my neck. I pulled the faucet handle towards me to splash my face with cold water. My fingers rubbed against each other under the flow coming from the sink. My fingers numbed up.

In letting go, we find.
This had to be the clue to finding the bomb.
I sighed. The challenge would soon be over.
I stared at the sink.

I had such an infatuation with water. I longed for the opposite of what haunted me: the fire that burned my mom's house down. My house down.

My fingers clasped over the item protruding out of my pocket.

In letting go, we find.
I lifted up Kace's jacket and pulled out the lighter from my pocket.

My eyes burned as I stepped outside. The fog had now reached to the little neighborhood the Queens had. I blinked, allowing the moisture in my eyes to seep out.

I dropped the jacket onto the woods next to Maybelle's house. I flicked the lighter to start it and I let it fall onto Maybelle's old house. The light flickered and danced over the jacket.

My eyes burned. I blinked away the smoke. Something fired up my nose. Acidic chlorine running through a nose at the pool. My chest heaved, holding me up as weight pulled my knees down.

Lying down on the floor never felt better.

The brick ground snagged on my clothing and felt heavy against my head. I gulped a breath in feeling the oxygen expand in my lungs. I let the lighter in my hand roll onto the ground, dropping my hand on the hard brick surface.

I could still smell the smoke as my eyes watered when they shut.

My head whirled as I hoisted myself back up. I had a weird dream during that forced sleep. I sat up, rubbing my hair as I tried to recall what I just saw.

I was walking to a house. Where I was walking from? I had no clue. I looked behind me and frowned.

The house was in smoke, but it wasn't my mom's house.

I scanned the area for police. None to be found. I squinted to view the house better.

I looked back again. The house in front was Elaine's. I could recognize it anywhere with its white exterior and extending arc over the doorway. The house in front of Elaine's was Spencer's. His house was more modern with a flat roof and dark color scheme.

But, evidently, it was on fire. I walked towards the house, but the ground seemed to move forwards.

I clutched my stomach as I doubled over. My knees scratched against a floor of rugged carpet. I looked up as I rubbed at my bruised knees. A few men in all-black suits sat in folding chairs.

They sat around a casket. The casket was beautiful, with dark cherry wood that stood out in the dark burgundy room. A bouquet of baby's breath and rose flowers was dropped beside the casket, the petals falling off onto the floor. I frowned as I walked past them and I screamed after I saw who was inside. I covered my mouth with the back of my hand.

Kace laid down in the casket, but he wasn't dead. He was cold and bloody. His eyes had deep purple rings surrounding them. Bruises covered his collarbone and hands. Skin was peeling off from the skin covering his joints.

The closer I walked to him, the louder he screamed.

A tall man stepped forward towards the other side of the casket. He rubbed at his eyes.

I stepped back. "Spencer?"

He looked up at me slightly, before dropping his head to carefully look at Kace.

Kace squirmed, digging his nails into the off-white fabric of the casket.

Spencer covered his mouth to stop the screaming.

But Kace wouldn't stop.

He'd never stop.

I shut my eyes tight as I blocked out the sound of Kace's voice.

Chapter Fifty-eight

Pathetic

I slammed my palms into the tiles below me. I turned quickly. I recognized the room. Lauren's prophecy once was hung up on one of these walls and she had given me Marissa's note in this very area. My eyes darted to my lap.

My arms flailed behind me as I shrieked. I wrapped my arms around my chest and took a deep breath in. There was a box with the words, "Careful! Explosives inside" written on it on my lap.

I looked in front of me. I paused. In front of me was the worst thing I could have ever seen. My chest heaved. I wanted to cry. I wanted to cry and never get up. My school ID. The same one Eurydice and her friend took from my pocket.

I didn't even know the name of Eurydice's friend.

The box was freakishly taped. Off-white masking tape covered the edges of the box which made it impossible to open with my bare hands.

My chest heaved as I slid the ID gently under the tape. I pulled the card up, the tape coming up with it.

I delicately reached into the box. My fingers quivered as I reached for the grenade.

My fingers brushed against the cool surface of the grenade, pausing at an indent on the side of it.

I carefully reached into my pocket, balancing the grenade on my other leg.

A USB had to be inserted into the section of the grenade and Kace had given me two. One was marked A and the other B.

I recognized that one would have to be used for the grenade and the other I could use to try to bring them back once Maybelle helps me bring back my mom.

But which USB was which? One had Kace's data and the other was Spencer's.

I stood up, carefully picking up the grenade.

Kace and I had a plan where I'd throw the grenade into the sea rather than the designated area in the Tech building.

Not that the Tech building was intact anyway.

I ran my tongue over my teeth as I looked down at the USBs.

The salty smell of seawater made my stomach churn. I needed to wrap things up quickly.

In Kace's head, he was always second. Spencer came first and Spencer was my priority.

However, Kace was a liar. But his truths were always eventually revealed.

Spencer still held a lie over my head. He had evidence regarding my mother's death and although the other Queens were informed, it wasn't their place to tell. Yet Spencer didn't give me any information on the topic. But if I could revive Spencer, he'd *have* to tell me. It would be my reward for saving his life.

Kace was pathetic. He begged me to save him and not Spencer because he knew I'd save Spencer.

I inserted USB B in the grenade.

Kace was *wrong*.

Chapter Fifty-nine

Spencer, the Hologram

Nerissa chose the wrong person to take out of school. I could not seem to figure out how the bomb worked. Or any bomb for that matter.

I obviously didn't think the bomb would activate right after I plugged the USB in. Because otherwise, I'd be dead.

I patted my arm, feeling the solidness of my skin. Definitely not dead yet.

Red digital lettering appeared on the pearly white covering of the bomb. Set to detonate on impact.

I felt the grenade fall from my hands and splash into the water. My stomach heaved.

I shrieked, feeling my head rub against the gritty sand that was once under my feet.

I hastily slapped what was in front of me. I coughed out as my ears felt like they were about to fall out from the pressure of the water. I couldn't hear anything besides the trembling of my chest.

I needed air.

A force pressed down on my neck and I squeezed my eyes shut and tried to peel its fingers off.

Fingers?

I forced my eyes open. My eyes burned, I could feel the saltwater surrounding my face.

I'd recognize his face anywhere. It was Spencer who had a hand around my throat and his fingers clasped on my wrist.

But this wasn't Spencer. The USB had created a hologram of him with all his documented facial features and combat methods.

Spencer, himself, had no reason to fight me, but this USB wanted me dead.

I clawed at Spencer's face, his skin feeling like plastic against my nails. It was impossible to hit him back. Neither my scratches nor my punches did nothing to him.

I needed to get his hand off my throat. I dug my nails into the skin of his palm that was exposed.

With the little air I had left out of my chest, I let out a whimper.

The challenge was over, why did I still have to fight for my life? After all I had done to stay alive, I was going to die just because I completed the challenge.

I tried to blink up, to open my eyes. All I could see was a foggy blue.

I let myself sink down, Spencer's grasp on me loosening.

Chapter Sixty

The Re-Death
of Spence

"You cheated, Mia."

"What?" I murmured out. I was so grateful that I could finally breathe.

But it didn't feel like I was breathing oxygen. My lungs didn't satisfyingly expand from an intake of air.

I was quite literally breathing nothing. I jolted up; the realization had brought me to my senses.

Where the hell was I? My fingers were all wrinkly from being underwater, but there was no force holding me down, like the pressure of High Tide's sea.

Not only was I breathing absolutely nothing, I was also in absolute nothingness.

I felt my chest heave out as if I was screaming, but no sound came out. I wiggled my arms, feeling two hands pushing me down. It was a gentle push as if someone were holding me steady.

Spencer's hair fell over his eyes as he held onto my arms.

"You're dead." My eyes widened. "But you're here." I looked down at my chest. "So, *I'm* dead."

"You're not dead," Spencer said collectedly. "Just hallucinating."

"Why would a hallucination tell me I'm hallucinating?" I pointed out.

Spencer frowned, pushing my hair behind my ear. "You're here because you never actually finished the challenge. You cheated."

"Kace," I realized. "He told me he'd steer the monsters away from me. I never actually fought any of the creatures, unless I was with you."

Spencer smiled smugly. "If you chose your little boyfriend to plug in the bomb, you wouldn't be here. He'd let you go free if he were in place of me."

"I can't control what Kace does."

Spencer pressed the tips of his fingers to my cheek. "So, you agree?" He paused. "You agree that you should have plugged him in and not me?"

"Is that what this is? You're jealous? How was I supposed to know which USB was which?"

Spencer looked away from me to laugh at himself. He leaned forward to speak to me directly. "You're too much like me. You wouldn't just *guess*. You *knew* you wanted to save Kace and not me."

I scoffed. "We are *nothing* alike. The non-hallucination version of you would agree as well."

Spencer cocked up an eyebrow and then shrugged. "You'd be surprised. I think our similarities were why we were friends." He bit down lightly on his tongue. "But it seems as if you don't want to be friends," he pouted sarcastically.

I pursed my lips as I shook my head at him out of disbelief. How could he be so childish?

His eyebrows pushed together as if he was recalling something. "You said I was jealous. I wanted what was best for you. If I was alive I could have told you the information I knew on your mother's death. We'd be friends, just like we once were."

I refused to look up at Spencer's face. "Then tell me what you know. You couldn't tell me before, so tell me now."

He reached his hand to the nape of my neck to force me to look up at him. His eyes were glassy and his cheeks were burning up, leaving a shade of red across his face.

"What don't you get, Mia?" He exhaled, "I'm *dead*. I can't tell you anything *because* I'm dead. *You* let me die for no reason." He sounded embarrassed. As if him dying meant he lost. Almost as if he believed that dying made him look weak.

His teeth clenched. His eyes darted down to his hand on my wrist and he let go to cup my face in his hands.

He whimpered, his voice cracking. "Did you ever care?"

"All I have been doing is caring about you, Spence."

A tear finally fell down from his face, I could feel his cool tears land on my cheeks. Spencer brushed them away carefully, his fingers tugging on my skin slightly. "I didn't want to die, Mia. I didn't want to die."

Chapter Sixty-one

The Wake

Spencer's vulnerability was short-lived as a laugh rang out. My knees buckled forward, but the same unpleasant feeling of nothing around me remained. My stomach churned. "Oh my god."

I'd seen my fair share of dead bodies in High Tide, but nothing like this. A woman in her late fifties was curled up under my feet. Her skin was dry, wrinkly—and *blue*. I gagged and looked up, not wanting to smell the rotting corpse. I squeezed my eyes shut before turning my head slightly to the right.

Blue-green hair. This old woman was *Marissa.*

I coughed, begging for something to hold onto as I tried to steady myself.

There were layers of dense fog surrounding me. The fog was visible, yet transparent.

I could see a body of water below me, but the rest was blurry from trying to blink out smoke.

My fists slammed against the aura around me.

Wake up.

Wake up.

I gasped. There was no waking up.

I'm dead. I drowned.

A man sighed behind me, resting his back against the aura.

"Spence?" I rasped out. He walked past me, remaining on my right side. His fingers brushed against the nape of my neck.

Spencer angled his head down to talk to me. "How many times do I have to tell you? You're not dead."

I looked down at the rock below me. I had fallen into the same fate as Marissa.

I was in the same aura she once was. I turned to Spencer to confirm my realization, but he had vanished.

The same laugh I heard before was audible again. I looked down.

Courtney leaned back and winked at me.

She mouthed, "Spencer's secret; you'll never know it." Maybelle was telling me about Spencer hiding something about my mother from me. But does that even matter now?

In Courtney's version of this story, she's the villain. She craved power, so she commanded it just like every villain ever.

But like Maybelle, she never was the evil one in this story.

Spencer craved power. I wasn't aware of it before, but I knew it now. Maybelle and Courtney were always open about their intentions, but I never knew what Spencer's motives were until it was too late.

The hallucination of Spencer had his hand on Courtney.

Spencer made one thing clear: he was all in my head. Courtney didn't even sense his presence.

But there was something extremely real in his hand.

Spencer grinned. "She's right."

Spencer raised his eyebrows at me and dangled the object towards me. The aura around me blocked me from moving as I lunged for what was in Spencer's hand.

A splash signified that the object had fallen into the water. With a jump, Courtney noticed that something had dropped in.

Kace's USB was in the water. Kace was officially dead. So, what now?

At the time, all I could feel was a lingering emptiness, but as I sit here and share my thoughts with you, I've come to a realization. I spent all of the High Tide Competition trying to figure people out. I did it out of safety. I needed to know what people's intentions were.

There were so many people I didn't want to be like. I feared I'd have the same fate as Courtney and Maybelle.

We think the immediate answer is to be ourselves and I tried that, but even Spencer thought I was as manipulative as him. Deep down, I know for sure that's not me. I am not manipulative, no matter what Spencer says.

If I can't be myself, then what can I be? Am I just nothing as I sit here with no intent?

If I have no reason for my existence then I, too, am as good as dead.

Epilogue

This is what was found in Spencer's pocket when he was taken into an Earth Hospital.

Dear Heir or Technician,

You've heard their stories, their mistakes, and the damage they did. But, there is another story that happened in the past you've only heard parts of.

So, now you understand, you've been through it. When you reached High Tide, you were either a Tech, a High Tide competitor, or an heir related to the current Queen(s). So far, there has been no King in High Tide.

However, whoever you are, High Tide is still dangerous, even if you escaped it. Take note of our mistakes. Don't make the same ones. Who knows? Maybe someday you'll be able to fix our mistakes for the better. Maybe someday High Tide wouldn't be such a dystopia. So I give you my best wishes. Good luck for the rest of your life, champion.

Yours truly,
Nerissa Young.

P.S. If you have found this, you have escaped. Congrats. And Maybelle would greatly appreciate it if you didn't send proof of High Tide's existence to the police. For no specific reason, of course.

Author's Note

I have been interested in creative writing since I was a young child. Most of my work has been poetry or short stories. High Tide is the first novel-length book I have written. Fifth grade me would be so proud of the fact that I have finally been able to publish my ideas into a physical book. I am so grateful for the opportunity to get my work published.

Sigma's Bookshelf (www.SigmasBookshelf.com) is an independent book publishing company that exclusively publishes the work of teenage authors, who are between the ages of 13 and 19. The company was founded in 2016 by Minnesota teenager Justin M. Anderson, whose first book, *Saving Stripes: A Kitty's Story*, was published when he was 14, and has since sold hundreds of copies.

"I know there are a lot of other teenagers out there who are good writers and deserve to have their work published, but don't have access to the kinds of resources I do. I wanted to help them," he said.

Sigma's Bookshelf is a sponsored project of Springboard for the Arts, a nonprofit arts service organization. Contributions on behalf of Sigma's Bookshelf may be made payable to Springboard for the Arts and are tax deductible to the extent permitted by law. Donations can be made online at www.SigmasBookshelf.com/donate.

www.ingramcontent.com/pod-product-compliance
Lightning Source LLC
Chambersburg PA
CBHW030819210726
48290CB00002B/667